TRADING FACES

Julia DeVillers
Jennifer Roy

ALADDIN

NEW YORK   LONDON   TORONTO   SYDNEY

ALADDIN
An imprint of Simon & Schuster Children's Publishing Division
1230 Avenue of the Americas, New York, NY 10020
Text copyright © 2009 by Julia DeVillers and Jennifer Roy
Cover illustration copyright © 2009 by Paige Pooler
All rights reserved, including the right of reproduction
in whole or in part in any form.
ALADDIN and related logo are registered trademarks
of Simon & Schuster, Inc.
Designed by Karin Paprocki
The text of this book was set in Granjon.
Manufactured in the United States of America
First Aladdin hardcover edition January 2009
4 6 8 10 9 7 5 3
Library of Congress Cataloging-in-Publication Data
The Library of Congress has cataloged the hardcover edition as follows:
DeVillers, Julia.
Trading faces / by Julia DeVillers and Jennifer Roy ; cover
illustrated by Paige Pooler.
p. cm.
Summary: When seventh-grade twins Payton and Emma switch
places, they shake up the social hierarchy at their new middle school.
ISBN-13: 978-1-4169-7531-1 (hardcover ed.)
ISBN-10: 1-4169-7531-4 (hardcover ed.)
[1. Twins—Fiction. 2. Sisters—Fiction. 3. Mistaken identity—Fiction.
4. Cliques (Sociology)—Fiction. 5. Middle schools—Fiction.
6. Schools—Fiction.] I. Roy, Jennifer Rozines, 1967- II. Title.
PZ7.D4974Tr 2009
[Fic]—dc22
2008021643

Dedicated to Adam Roy and Jack DeVillers—
"sort of" identical twin cousins

Payton

One

FIRST DAY OF SCHOOL, BEFORE HOMEROOM

Lip gloss! Oh, no—did I forget my lip gloss?

I opened my tote bag and scrounged around in a panic. I felt my brush and mirror. My lunch. My lunch money in case buying lunch was cooler than packing. Ouch, sharp pencil. And . . . yeesh! I felt my lip gloss.

Phew, I'd remembered everything. Everything important for the first day of school, that is.

THE FIRST DAY OF SCHOOL! THE FIRST DAY OF SEVENTH GRADE!!!

I was seriously excited. I'd spent the last six years in a small girls' school. And by small I mean there was only one class in each grade. It was the same people over and

 1

over every year. But not this year . . . because I was switching to public school! Heck yeah, I was psyched. Switching classes! Different teachers! After-school activities! My own locker! New people! CUTE GUYS!

"This school is so huge!" I said. It looked like any old big building. Lots of bricks and windows. But it wasn't just any old building. It was middle school. *My* middle school.

"Look, Emma!" I pointed to the banner saying WELCOME! that was draped over the main entrance. "How nice and welcomey!"

"'Welcomey' is not a word," said my sister. *Great.* "And I hardly call this factory-like architecture welcoming."

I ignored my sister. No one was going to bring me down today! Even the earliness of the school day—which meant I'd had to get up at six in the morning—wasn't as tragic as I'd expected. I'd been too excited to sleep, anyway.

THE FIRST DAY OF SCHOOL! THE FIRST DAY OF SEVENTH GRADE!

!!!!!!!!!!!!!!!!!!

I let out a squeal of pure excitement.

At the exact same moment I heard a big sigh.

2

It came from my twin sister, Emma, who was walking next to me. We had gotten off the bus and were now walking up the sidewalk to our NEW SCHOOL!

"Are you thinking what I'm thinking?" Emma asked me.

"You're thinking how cool it will be to have nine different classes each day?" I asked her. "Different teachers to break up the boredom? Cheerleading tryouts, student council, and our very own lockers to decorate? Hundreds of new people to meet? Millions of cute guys?"

"Well, no," Emma said. "Actually, not even close."

Whoever said identical twins can read each other's minds wasn't talking about us. I followed Emma as she maneuvered around tons of people. The sidewalk was getting more and more crowded as we got closer to the school. I watched a girl run over to a group of people. They were so happy to see her that they swallowed her up in a group hug.

Maybe soon that would be me: a girl with friends at school who were happy to see her.

"Hello? Earth to Payton?" Emma said to me. "Don't you want to know what I was thinking?"

"Oh, sure," I said, turning back toward my sister. "What were you thinking?"

"I was thinking about how many millions of times we're going to get the question," Emma said. "You just *know* we're going to be getting the question."

I had to agree with her there. She was right. I knew exactly what she meant by the question:

"Which one are you?"

Whenever we'd meet new people, they couldn't tell us apart. So they'd double-check: "Which one are you?" And I'd have to answer, "I'm Payton, not Emma."

Everyone in elementary school was used to us. But even then they mixed us up sometimes. And yeah, it got annoying. Seriously, I thought it was pretty obvious which one I was. I mean, I'm an inch taller than Emma. My eyes are a teeny bit greener. I definitely have shinier hair.

But okay, we'd always looked pretty much exactly the same.

If only we didn't look *so* much alike. If we looked even a little different, it would make life a lot easier. I'd tried to talk her into cutting her hair short, but she refused. She'd told me that if I wanted to look different so badly, I could cut *my* hair.

Psshh. I wasn't going to cut *my* hair, that was for sure. It was my best feature. Long, brownish-blond—and like I said, shiny.

"There's Margaret from the state spelling bee!" Emma said. Then she yelled, "Margaret! Spell 'corpuscle'!"

Loudly enough for the people nearby to give us a weird look. Could you believe this? This was so not the attention I was looking for.

"Margaret!" she said, a little louder. "Corpuscle!"

I elbowed Emma to stop with the screeching. She couldn't read my mind, but I was sure she could read my elbow jab.

"Why did you jab me?" Emma asked.

Or not.

"Stop yelling," I whispered. "People are looking at you."

"They are not," Emma said loudly. "Don't be paranoid."

I leaned over to see if anyone else was looking at her. I guess not. Everyone was too busy reuniting with their friends. I watched two tan girls hug each other. They were dressed like twins, in matching brown shirts, jeans, and cute flats. I looked around and saw more girls in jeans.

I looked down at my skirt. Uh-oh. Maybe I made a mistake not wearing jeans. I elbowed Emma again.

"What *now?*" she said. "I'm not making any noise!"

"I know," I whispered. "Um, it's just . . . do you think my outfit's okay?"

Emma sighed.

"For the thousandth time, yes," Emma said. "Your outfit is fine."

"Everyone's wearing jeans," I said. "But Ashlynn said skirts were totally in for the first day of school!"

"Oh, no," Emma groaned. "I thought after camp was over I'd never have to hear the name Ashlynn again."

Emma and I had gone to sleepaway camp for the first time this summer. Ashlynn, the girl who slept in the bunk under me, was from New York City. Even though the brochure had said to bring our grossest clothes to camp, Ashlynn had ignored that. We only have one mall in our town, so everyone here dresses pretty much the same. But at camp people came from different cities, and everyone was always gushing over Ashlynn's cool outfits. So I did Ashlynn's bunk chores as a trade for her clothes. While Ashlynn worked on her tan, I suffered through cleaning the bathroom, sweeping the bunk, and doing her kitchen-duty.

Emma called them my Summer Slave clothes.

"You know how they say some girls are slaves to fashion? Well, you were really a slave!" she said. She called them my Summer Slave clothes so many times, I couldn't help thinking of them that way too.

I'd made Ashlynn's bed for a week for the skirt I was wearing today. I looked down at the outfit I'd carefully picked out. I was wearing:

☑ Denim miniskirt with the logo on the pocket
(Summer Slave clothes)

☑ A pale pink tank with lace and sequins on it
(Summer Slave clothes)

☑ A medium-sleeved gray V-neck hoodie
(Summer Slave too)

☑ A pink and blue beaded necklace
(Summer Slave again)

☑ Pink flip-flops with a little gray in them
(Yes, Summer Slave. A little too big, but too cool not to wear.)

I stood up straight and tried to walk confidently. My skirt, tank, and hoodie were TC Couture. Ashlynn said TC Couture stood for Tragically Cute and promised that if I wore it I'd be a totally trendy fashionista.

Please let me look cute. And not tragic.

"You're fine," Emma reassured me. "Stop worrying about your outfit."

Okay. I was too excited to stay worried long. The first day of school was always so bright and shiny. The walls were still white with fresh paint, and I could feel the bottoms of my flip-flops squeak against the newly waxed floor.

We walked down a hallway. I followed Emma. She'd memorized the map of our school so we'd know where to go. Which was crucial, because I get totally lost really easily.

Ugh. My pink tank top felt weird. I stopped for a second, shrugging my shoulders to subtly adjust the tank-top strap.

"Payton, keep up with me!" Emma looked back at me. "Why are you wiggling around like that?"

"I'm not wiggling!" I said. I hurried to catch up with her. Except that as I walked, my tank top felt like it was sliding down for some reason. I switched my tote bag to my other shoulder and shrugged again.

"Yes, you are!" Emma said, loudly. "You're wiggling! Synonyms: 'squirming' and 'writhing.'"

"Will you shush already?" I hissed. And then all of a

sudden I felt something whip me across the face.

"OW!" I yelped. Total whiplash across my face! *What the heck was*—and then I felt my tank top slide completely down my shoulder and down my front and—

Oh, my gosh! My tank-top strap attacked me! The elastic must have broken and whiplashed me!

"Payton? Are you having a seizure?" Emma asked me.

"Don't make a scene, but there's an emergency," I said in a strangled voice. "My tank-top strap broke."

"Gotcha," Emma said, looking around. "Look, there's a closet. Quick, Payton! Inside!"

I followed Emma quickly as she opened a door.

"It's empty," she whispered to me, shoving me inside.

I looked around. It was pretty dark in there with the door shut, but I could barely make out a bucket, a smelly mop—I was in a janitor's closet. Swell. I took my hoodie off and pulled the tank top back up. I tried to tie it, but I couldn't get it to stay. I thought about just ripping it off and stuffing the tank in my tote bag, but no—my hoodie was too low in front to wear alone. Help!

"Emma!" I knocked on the closet door. It opened a crack.

"What?" Emma stuck her head in.

"I can't get my tank-top strap to stay tied!" I told her.

The door closed. What? Was Emma leaving me in my time of need? Then the door opened and Emma's head reappeared. She tossed something into the closet. I heard it roll across the floor.

"Duct tape!" Emma said. "I always keep some in my backpack in case of emergency. Here are some safety scissors to cut it off the roll. Did you know that duct tape was first invented in World War Two to help the American military—"

"SHUT THE DOOR!" I hissed at her. *AGH!* "I'm half dressed!"

The door shut. Now where was that duct tape? I felt around on the floor in the semi-darkness. Ew, gross—there was a puddle on the floor. And then I felt the roll of duct tape. I ripped off a piece and wrapped it around the broken strap. I tugged on it. It felt like it would hold. Fortunately it had broken near the bottom, so it wouldn't show under my hoodie. It wasn't the most comfortable feeling, but . . . I was back in action.

Alrighty, then. I picked up my tote bag and tried to open the door. It wouldn't open.

"Emma! Let me out!" I knocked on the door.

"Not yet," I heard Emma whisper. "People are going by. . . . Okay, you're clear! Come out now!"

I exited the closet smoothly, as if nothing had happened. *La la la . . . Nobody noticed me, right? Nobody saw an identical twin hopping out of the janitor's closet. And um, nobody witnessed my tank top attacking me, did they?*

Right? RIGHT?

"How ironic is it that the outfit you slaved for falls apart the first day of school?" Emma said, starting to walk down the hall again.

"I am proud to suffer for fashion," I said, scratching at the duct tape. Unlike some *other* person I knew. I looked at Emma's T-shirt and track pants. Now it was my turn to sigh. Emma was slightly fashion-challenged. I'd been trying to help her pick a good outfit for weeks now. Last night I had given it one last-ditch effort.

"So what are you wearing tomorrow?" I'd asked Emma.

"Oh, I still don't know," Emma said. "You know I don't care about any of that."

"Emma, you have to care!" I pleaded. "It's the first day at our new school!"

"I'll find something." Emma had kept waving me off.

I wish she'd at least have let me pick something out

for her. Not only because I was concerned about Emma's image, but for my sake too. People mixed us up all the time. What if people thought she was me?

Anyway, I think we really were starting to look different. This summer at camp, I felt like I'd matured a little bit. Maybe people would at least think I was the older twin!

Everyone always asked us which one was older. The answer was Emma. She is six minutes older than me. Who knows, maybe people wouldn't even think we were twins. *They might think I'm the older sister!*

"Whoa." A guy passed us and turned around to look at us again. He was kind of cute. "Are you two twins?"

"Yes!" I said. I smiled what I hoped was a friendly, slightly flirty smile. Emma just turned purple, like she always does when a guy talks to her.

"Freakish," he said, shaking his head and continuing down the hallway.

My smile faded. Did he just say 'freakish'? Weird. I followed Emma, who started walking again.

"And so it begins," Emma said. "Our first twin question of middle school."

And not the last, I was sure. I saw a girl turn around and do a double take at us.

Emma and I walked on. Past a case full of trophies,

past a boys' bathroom. *Heh*. That made me remember something funny.

"Remember that first day of kindergarten, when you got the doors to the boys' and girls' bathrooms mixed up?" I asked Emma. "And you walked in on Joseph Jones when he was going to the bathroom?"

"Don't bring that up!" she said. "I'm trying to block that out of my memory! I was traumatized! What a way to start my school career."

"Well, I just started my middle-school career in a janitor's closet being attacked by my tank top," I whispered. "And now I've been forced to embellish my carefully chosen outfit with duct tape."

"Maybe you got yours over with and I'm still going to have my embarrassing moment," Emma said. "Payton, I'm kind of worried about today."

I already knew this. When Emma gets worried, which is like, always, she does this thing with her hair. She chews on the ends until they get all soggy.

"Okay, I'll give you some important advice." I leaned over like I was going to tell her a big secret. She looked at me hopefully.

"The boys' room will say 'Boys' on it," I said. "Use the *other* one."

Hee.

"Gee, thanks, Payton," Emma said. "While we're on the topic of first days, shall I remind you about the first day of fifth grade, when you burped in class?"

No. That was bad. One minute I was sitting all nicely, making a good first-day impression. And the next minute . . .

WUUUURP.

I'd burped loudly enough for even our teacher to crack up laughing. *Augh.* Nervous stomach. I reminded myself to avoid that issue and not to drink soda today.

I followed Emma around a corner and up some stairs.

"Be careful on the steps." Emma turned around to warn me. "Remember when you missed a step in third grade and knocked down the class like dominoes?"

I shuddered. That was bad. First one of my classmates went down. Then four more. *Boom. Boom boom boom boom.*

And then our teacher. *Crash.*

"Okay, okay," I groaned. "No more school embarrassing moments."

And I was determined that there would be no more in my future. I stood up straighter and did my best to look confident. I was going to be the new improved middle-school Payton! This time we were going down some stairs, and I gracefully walked down them without tripping even once.

"It was amazing you were as popular as you were," Emma said thoughtfully.

"Can we stop this conversation now?" I said.

"That just shows how great your personality is, that you overcame such humiliations," Emma said.

"Thanks," I said. *I think?*

I followed Emma down the hall. All seventh-grade students (us!) were supposed to go to the gym and get their class schedules. I couldn't wait to get my new schedule! Would there be nice people in my classes? Would I get gym last period so I wouldn't have to walk around sweaty all day? Would I get good teachers?

"I wonder how many classes we're going to be in together?" Emma asked me.

"Probably all of them. It would be too weird not to be in a class with you," I said. Since there was only one class in each grade at our old school, we'd always been in the same class. It had worked out great. On our report cards it always said something about how we each had our own strengths and yet we complemented each other. My mom said that meant we were different learners who made a nice team. Team Mills ruled elementary school!

Every year we'd be put in our seats with Emma in front, because she preferred to be as close to the teacher as possible. It was good Emma was there. A lot of the time I was spacing out or doodling, so Emma blocked me from the teacher's view. That made it easy. It was also hard because Emma was the Mills twin who always knew the answer. But it was also good because Emma never made me feel bad about it and could always help me with my homework. So it was good and bad and—

"Payton! PAYTON!" Emma snapped me out of it. "We're here!" She pointed to a sign on the gym that said 7TH GRADERS!

We walked into the gym and went to the L-M-N-O line. As I waited, I looked around the gym. I looked at the GO GECKOS pennants hanging on the walls. I pictured myself wearing a green and white cheerleader outfit and jumping around the gym with my new BFF cheerleader friends.

Then Emma poked me in the back. *Oh!* It was my turn!

"Name?" the woman behind the table asked.

"Payton Mills," I announced. She handed me a sheet of paper. I looked at it while Emma was getting hers.

Yeesh! Last-period PE! Awesome! First-period study hall, second-period Science—

"Let's get to homeroom," Emma said. "The lady said Room 224 is down the hall to the left."

"You mean Room 220, to the right," I said.

"No, Room 224," Emma said. She double-checked her card. She took my card. "Wait a minute—we're in different homerooms? But homeroom is alphabetical!"

I looked at both cards. 220. 224.

Then we both realized. We'd been split up.

"It'll be okay," I reassured her. "We'll be together for . . ."

"For nothing," Emma said, handing me our schedules. "Look! We don't have any classes together, Payton. NOT EVEN LUNCH!"

Emma spoke so loudly, people nearby turned around.

I heard the girl standing next to me say, "Did you see those twins? They look *exactly* alike!"

"Yeah," another girl answered. "Except that one has a bigger nose."

I self-consciously covered my nose. Okayyy . . . maybe separate classrooms wasn't such a bad idea.

And then the homeroom bell went off. Everyone

started moving out of the gym to start their day. I was so excited. This was it! I looked at Emma. Time to say good-bye for now and Hellooo, middle school!

I reached out my hand to Emma. "Twins rule!" I said, as we did our twin hand-slap. We high-fived, low-fived, bumped fists . . .

I waved to Emma and headed out the gym door. And turned right. And Emma turned left.

Emma

Two

FIRST DAY OF SCHOOL, BEFORE HOMEROOM

Calculator! Did I forget my calculator? I opened my backpack and searched. I felt my planner, my bag lunch . . . ouch! Sharp compass . . . and there it was. My calculator.

Okay, I was prepared for the first day of school. The first day of seventh grade.

I was so, so nervous.

I wish it were last year. I loved our small school: I knew everybody, and I knew what to expect. Everything was under control. In elementary school I knew who I was. Emma the Brain. Emma the Achiever. Emma with the near-photographic memory. But in middle school there would be kids from all over. Smart, talented students. More competition. The pressure would be ON. This middle school was huge. It had three stories and four wings. I'd looked at the website and found out there were 655 seventh graders and 710 eighth graders.

$$
\begin{array}{r}
655 \\
+710 \\
\hline
1365
\end{array}
$$

$$- (\text{me} + \text{Payton}) = 1363$$

1363 total strangers in this school!

I shuddered. How would I stand out in such a massive group? By studying. Preparing. Competing. And winning.

"Ugh," I said out loud.

At that exact same moment I heard an excited squeal. I looked at my twin sister, Payton, walking next to me on our way into our new school.

"Are you thinking what I'm thinking?"

Payton started going on and on about how cool and exciting our new school was going to be. Sometimes I can't believe we're even related. Of course, everyone else can believe it. It's totally obvious, since we're identical twins.

"Don't you want to know what I was thinking?" I interrupted her. I'd never get a chance to speak otherwise.

"Oh, sure," Payton said, obviously not really paying attention. "What were you thinking?"

"I was thinking about how many millions of times we're going to get the question," I said. "You just know we're going to be getting the question."

The question: Which one are you?

The answer: I'm Emma. I'm not Payton. I'm Emma. Emma. Emma. Emma. I am first in alphabetical order. I'm one-half inch shorter. And I have a freckle on my cheek near my left ear. It is my most obvious difference from my twin sister. Although my hair covers it up mostly, so everyone thinks we are 100 percent identical. Payton has been trying to convince me to cut my hair. I am NOT cutting my hair. No way. My hair is my best feature. It's easy to just brush straight and go. No fuss. No stress.

I wish the rest of my life were so stress-free.

"Stop making that noise," Payton whispered. "Those girls are looking at you!"

What noise? I was just calling to my friend. Oh,

please, like people would really be looking at me. All I saw were girls we didn't know who were acting all huggy and cutesy. But oh, there was a girl who looked familiar.

"There's Margaret from the state spelling bee!" I said. "Hey, Margaret! Spell 'corpuscle'!"

'Corpuscle' was a word that Margaret had spelled correctly during the last round of the bee. But Margaret didn't hear me. There were too many people around.

"Margaret!" I called out. "Corpuscle!"

Ow again. Would Payton stop elbowing me?

"Why did you jab me?" I said.

"People are looking at you," Payton whispered.

"What people?" Payton could be so paranoid. Rats, Margaret had disappeared into the squish of people. Hopefully I'd see her in one of my advanced classes. Anyone who could spell 'pyrrhic' I'd like to get to know better.

The main entrance had led us into the front lobby. Lots of people were walking around. I looked up. The ceiling was two stories high. And bright green. A green ceiling? There were two sets of stairs—one to the left, one to the right. The railings were painted in green and white stripes.

"What's with all the green?" I said.

"Green and white are our school colors," Payton told me impatiently. "Don't you know anything?"

Apparently not. I'd memorized an entire atlas, a dictionary, and the world almanac. But in middle school what you needed to know about was our middle school.

"And our rivals are the Red Raiders," Payton said. "Boo, Raiders!"

Then she elbowed me . . . *again*.

"Emma," Payton whispered. "Um, it's just . . . do you think my outfit's okay?"

Not THIS again.

"For the thousandth time, yes," I told her. "Your outfit is fine." Payton shifted around, looking uncomfortable in her outfit. She pulled on the neck of her hoodie, which must have been tight. *I bet she wishes she wore comfy track pants and her lucky T-shirt like I did.*

"Everyone's wearing jeans," Payton said. "But Ashlynn said skirts were totally in for the first day of school."

"Oh, no," I groaned. "I thought after camp was over I'd never have to hear the name Ashlynn again."

I called Payton's clothes Summer Slave clothes. She'd worked like a slave all summer, and for what? So she could look like some girl, Ashlynn. Ridiculous.

Payton hadn't always been so clothes clothes clothes.

❀ 23 ❀

But at camp she was put in a cabin with girls who called themselves 'fash.' So here we are, out in the forest supposed to be bonding with nature, and Payton becomes obsessed with clothes instead. I was in the Purple Pandas. All the Pandas were into the real camp experience. Hiking, swimming, canoeing. Except one Panda: me.

I really don't like the outdoors. I couldn't care less who captured the flag or won camp spirit. So I told my counselor I had a pollengenic allergy. She said she knew I'd made that up. So I offered to write the camp newspaper. Since my counselor was supposed to write the newspaper, she cheerfully agreed that my allergy should keep me inside. I wrote; she spent time with her boyfriend at the boys' camp. The Purple Pandas (minus me) had their total camp experience. I gained journalism experience.

Anyway, I like to write. And I knew it would look good when I tried out for the school newspaper. I hope I make the school newspaper. *I hope I make the mathletics and the Scrabble-lympics teams.*

Honestly, what I really hoped was to make it through the first day of school. I was putting on a brave face, but inside, my stomach was in knots.

Nervous? Yes. Nauseous? Check.

Oh. I'd just twisted and chewed my hair into a soggy

knot. I smoothed down my hair and smiled my "confident" smile. The smile I'd practiced and used to intimidate not only Margaret, but also Clark and Dimitri at the spelling bee. Hee hee. The smile had worked. I came in first.

"Emma, why are you baring your teeth like a mad cat?" Payton asked me.

I stopped with the smile. At least I was confident about where we were going. I had memorized the map of our school so we'd know where to go. We walked down the main hallway. There were signs and posters up on the walls. Good. They gave me something to look at besides all these people.

MAKE THIS YEAR THE BEST YEAR!

OUR SCHOOL ROCKS!

GECKOS RULE!

GECKOS ARE #1!

Some of the signs showed our school mascot.

"Our school mascot is a gecko?" I mused aloud. Interesting. Not.

SUPER SCIENTISTS CLUB! WEDNESDAYS AT 3.
MEET IN LAB A.

Interesting, yes!

I'd be there! I made a mental note to write down the info in my planner.

Walking . . . bumping . . . jostling. Could there be any more people crushed into the hallway? Wasn't there a fire code about this? I kept hold of Payton's bag so I wouldn't lose her in the crowd. Another poster:

SOCCER TRYOUTS. BOYS: WEDNESDAY AT 3.
GIRLS: THURSDAY AT 3.

Emma + any kind of ball = total humiliation. No soccer for *moi*. I sped past that one.

"Payton, keep up with me!" I turned and looked at her. She had slowed down. She was tugging at her hoodie again. *Hurry up!* Why was she wiggling and squirming and writhing and holding me up on our first day of school? Was Payton sick?

"Are you having a seizure?" I asked her.

Now I was concerned. My sister wouldn't risk making a scene in school unless there was an emergency.

"Don't make a scene, but there's an emergency," Payton whispered. "My tank-top strap broke."

Oh. I spotted a closet.

"Quick, Payton! Inside!"

She went in and pulled the door closed. I stood outside the door, blocking it so no one could try to go in.

No one was trying to go in. They were all going where they were supposed to. Except me, just standing there like a statue.

La la la. I tried to look casual, like I was doing this on purpose. I opened up my backpack and looked inside. Ahhh, the scent of fresh school supplies. I'd alphabetized my folders: English, math, science . . . everything was perfect.

Tap, tap. Tap. Payton was knocking on the closet door. She peeked out.

"What?" I stuck my head in. *Whew. Pungent.*

"I can't get my tank-top strap to stay tied!" Payton said.

Hmm . . . I could take care of that. I pushed the door closed and felt around in the "supplies" compartment of my backpack. There it was! Duct tape!

I opened the closet door and tossed it in. I began explaining the wonders of duct tape, but Payton yelled at me to shut the door. I shut the door. Fine. Some people didn't appreciate good trivia.

"Do you need some help finding your way?" A woman's voice boomed loudly through the halls.

I looked up into the face of a teacher. Like all the

adults in the building, she had a security ID tag dangling from her neck. I quickly scanned it: MRS. BURKLE. FACULTY. ENGLISH DEPARTMENT.

"Um, er, no," I stammered. "I'm okay." *Please leave, please leave*, I thought. I leaned against the closet door so Payton wouldn't pop out unexpectedly.

"Do you need help with directions?" the teacher asked, so loudly that people turned around to look at us.

Need help with directions? Me? I was the one who'd memorized the map and had every hallway timed to the second. Payton was the one who needed help. Even getting dressed. What was taking her so long?

"No, thank you," I said. "I'm, uh, just resting."

"Resting!" Mrs. Burkle said. "You're already tired on the first day of school? This is why I think daily about retiring! Students today have no motivation! It's a disgrace! Young lady, I implore you to think about the importance of not being . . . what do you young people call it these days? A slacker!"

A slacker? She thinks *I'm* a slacker? Me? A teacher thinks Emma Mills, spelling-bee champion/mathlete/science-fair winner/straight-A student/teacher's pet, could possibly be a slacker?

She peered at me closely.

❁ 28 ❁

"If you're in my class this year, I hope you improve your attitude," the teacher said.

Emergency! A teacher has a negative first impression of me!

"Hello! It's nice to meet you!" I said, in a desperate attempt to improve my image. "I'm—"

"Ew." Mrs. Burkle wrinkled her nose.

What?

"Something smells horrible," she said, backing away as if it were me. "I must get to my classroom."

Augh! I slumped back against the closet door and—

Ew. Something did smell awful. The smell was coming from inside the closet. What was in there anyway? I stepped back and saw a sign I hadn't noticed before: JANITOR.

Uh-oh! Payton was in the janitor's closet? She wasn't going to be too happy about this. PU, that was some stench. I stepped away from the door to get some fresh air, and—*boom!* I stepped right into the path of a girl carrying a large musical-instrument case.

Oh. No. It was like slow motion. I watched as the contents of my unzipped backpack flew through the air. My folders! My mechanical pencils! *Oh, noooo!* I bent down and tried not to get stepped on as I scooped up my supplies. There was no time to reorganize. I just had to stuff everything into my backpack.

Grr. This was *so* Payton's fault.

"Emma!" I heard Payton's muffled voice. "Let me out!"

I couldn't reach the doorknob from my crouching position on the floor.

"Not yet! People are going by!" I lied. I jumped up and zipped my backpack. "Okay, you're clear."

She came out. I gave her a look.

"How ironic is it that the outfit you slaved for falls apart the first day of school?" I asked her. There. That would teach her a lesson to stop focusing on trivial stuff like clothes and fashion. And ruining my whole first-day-of-school organization plan. Gosh, I was so much more mature than Payton. No wonder I was six minutes older.

A boy walked past us and stopped.

"Whoa," he said. The boy looked at both of us. "Are you two twins?"

"Yes!" Payton said, smiling a weird grin.

"Freakish," he said. Then he was gone.

"And so it begins," I said. "Our first twin question of middle school."

We walked past a case full of trophies. I vowed to

add to that collection. Then we passed the boys' bathroom. *Oh, no. I just remembered something.* I looked at Payton, and she was smiling.

Payton, don't even go there.

"Remember that first day of kindergarten, when you got the doors to the boys' and girls' bathrooms mixed up?" she said. "And you walked in on Joseph Jones when he was going into the bathroom?"

Ugh. Ugh. Ugh. She went there.

Thanks, Payton. I'm nervous enough without remembering my past school trauma. *Do not show weakness!* I told myself.

Here's a secret: I was so scared about being in a class without Payton. Of course, she never helped me with schoolwork. And I was looking forward to being in advanced classes instead of just doing advanced work in a class with everyone else. (Joke!) But . . . (this is embarrassing) when Payton is in my class, then I can count on having at least one friend. So the more classes we have together the better.

Uh, not like I didn't have friends at my old school. Well, friend. Lakisha and I had study dates at each other's houses on a regular basis. And it wasn't all work and no play. We mixed in some Othello and snacks, too.

But having my sister around always makes my life easier.

The Payton Advantage:
- ❀ If I get too serious, she knows how to crack me up.
- ❀ She invites me into her group of friends so I never have to feel left out.

Another thing I can count on from Payton is reassurance. She understands me. So if I tell her I'm a little nervous, she'll say something like, *Silly Emma. You'll have nothing to worry about. You'll be the school genius, as always, and everyone will admire you.*

"Payton, I'm kind of worried about today," I said.

"Okay," Payton said seriously. "I'll give you some important advice."

See? I knew I could count on her.

"The boys' room will say 'Boys' on it," she said. "Use the *other* one."

Oh, ha ha. Very amusing. Shall I remind Payton of her past fiascos? Yes. I shall. The Great Burp of Fifth Grade. The Third-Grade Stairs Incident. The—

❀ 32 ❀

"Okay, okay!" she laughed. "No more school embarrassing moments!"

Past, present, or future, I hoped. Moving onward. Down these stairs and around the corner should be the gym. I slowed down on the stairs, just to be on the safe side, so Payton wouldn't trip and fall again. Payton followed me down the hall and around the corner. And then—

I saw it. On the wall. A sign.

103! 23! GET **PRIMED** FOR MATHLETICS!
STAY 2NED FOR MORE DATA!
DATE, TIME & PLACE 2 BE ANNOUNCED!

Hee hee! Primed? 103 and 23 are prime numbers. *Those mathletes are so hilarious. I'm definitely going to be there.* Clubs don't start until the third week of school, the school manual had said. How could I wait that long? Well, it'll give me extra time to prepare. I also planned to join GeoBee and Spelling Bee and Science Olympiad. Woo-hoo!

We walked a little further and then . . .

"Payton," I said. "PAYTON! We're here!"

The gym was filled with students anxiously awaiting their schedules. We walked over and stood in the

L-M-N-O line. Payton got in front of me. As I waited, I thought about how important this moment was. My schedule would organize my life for a whole school year. What if I had Math first period? That would be so great. I'd be bouncing into school each morning. Although if it were last, I could look forward to it all day! And Science? Woo-hoo! I'll take that any time of day. Thinking about my favorite classes started to cheer me up.

We reached the table. This was it. The moment of truth. Well, first it would be Payton's moment of truth. I poked her in the back.

While Payton got her schedule, I looked around. I saw Ahmad from the robotics tournament! And I recognized a girl I'd seen in the paper winning the Young Scientist Challenge. Jazmine something. Her science was pretty impressive, but I bet I could have beaten her. Gosh, I wished that the science challenge hadn't been the same day as the spelling bee. It had looked like a blast.

I'd never spoken to these people before. They'd always been on other school teams. They'd been the competition. That would all change this year! We were all on the same team now. This was great! I almost felt a little popular.

"Emma Mills," I said to the lady behind the table, after Payton had stepped away. The woman handed me my schedule and gave me directions to homeroom.

"Let's get to homeroom," I said, checking the clock. We only had three minutes to get there. We could compare schedules on the way.

"The lady said room 224 is down the hall to the left," I told Payton, starting to head out of the gym.

"You mean Room 220, to the right," she said.

What? I double-checked my card. Then I looked at Payton's.

"We're in different homerooms?" I tried not to panic. "But homeroom is alphabetical!"

We'd been split up. Okay. Okay. I'd handle different homerooms. I looked at the schedule. Homeroom was only fifteen minutes.

"It'll be okay." Payton tried to make me feel better. "We'll be together for . . ."

I consulted the schedule. WHAT?!

"For nothing!" I said. No classes together? "NOT EVEN LUNCH!" I wailed.

"Did you see those twins?" some girl said. "They look *exactly* alike."

Now people were staring at us.

"Yeah," another girl said. "Except that one has a bigger nose."

Oh, boy. It was true. Payton got the nose. I got the ears. I patted down my hair to cover them.

Clang! The bell.

I couldn't hear anything Payton was saying.

"Payton, I can't hear you amidst this chaos," I said.

Then I saw her hand reach out. I smiled. Our twin hand-slap. We high-fived, low-fived, bumped fists . . .

Then I took a deep breath. We had to go. I watched Payton turn around and leave. I headed out the gym door after her.

And turned left.

Payton

Three

HOMEROOM

I was the last person, alphabetically, in Homeroom 220, which put me in the last seat in the last row. This was my favorite place to sit. I could hide from the teacher and scope out everything going on in front of me.

But this was just homeroom, so it didn't really matter much. It's not like the teacher was going to call on me to answer anything I couldn't handle.

"Mills, Payton?" the teacher called out.

"Here!" I said. See? That's the kind of question I don't mind if teachers call on me for. But usually I hate when teachers call on me. And if I felt pressured before in school, then I really felt pressure now. Because for the first time Emma wasn't in my classes. Before, if a teacher called on me and I didn't know the answer, Emma was always there to wave her hand around and rescue me.

I had no one to rescue me now.

"Mills, Payton? Mills, are you here?" the teacher was saying.

Huh?

"Yeah!" I said, holding up my hand. "Yeah, I'm here!"

"Next time, please speak up when I call on you," the teacher said. "Or you'll be marked absent."

Okay, great. Apparently, I had to feel pressured even getting called on for attendance. People turned around to look at me, but they lost interest and went back to what they were doing.

I positioned myself behind the person in front of me so the teacher wouldn't notice me again. The girl in front of me had seriously great hair. I thought my hair was shiny, but hers was like a shampoo commercial. It was long, and razor sharp at the ends.

The girl turned around and passed back an envelope with my name on it.

"Thanks!" I said with what I hoped was a friendly but cool smile that would lead to her introducing herself. We'd talk a little bit, walk to our next class together, date best friends . . .

The girl turned back around.

Or she could turn back around and blow me off.

I busied myself opening the envelope. It had my locker number in it, 33638 and my combination, 18-25-22. Great, because I seriously needed to put my things in my locker. I hoped I had time before my next class.

I pulled out the school map and my schedule. I was in luck! My locker was in this hallway, and so was my study hall!

SCHEDULE Payton Mills			Grade 7
Period	Subject	Teacher	Room
Homeroom	–	Galbreath	220
1	Study Hall	–	245
2	Science	Carlson	227
3	French 1	Singer	130
4	Social Studies	Schain	136
5	Lunch	–	Cafeteria
6	ELA	Burkle	266
7	Math	Clifton	205
8	Art 1	Rigazio	099
9	PE/Wellness	Hoen	Gym 1

Study hall being first was excellent, because I could do any last-minute homework. And even more excellent, PE was last! That was major—I wouldn't have to feel sweaty all day.

I looked at my locker combination: 18-25-22. There was no way I'd remember that. I'd write it somewhere I wouldn't lose it, like . . . um, not on my hand . . . on my shoe. I took out a gel pen and wrote it along the side of my flip flop: 18-25-22.

I stuck my foot out to check it out. But I accidentally kicked the tote bag of the girl in front of me, and my flip-flop flew off.

The girl turned around and looked at me.

"Um, sorry," I said. "I'll just pick that up."

I leaned over to grab my shoe.

"That's cute," the girl said. She looked me up and down. "And that's a cute skirt, too. Where did you get it?"

Well. Actually, I got it after I swept our cabin like Cinderella, but I didn't think that was the right response.

"It's from a boutique in New York City," I told her.

The girl nodded. She didn't turn back around, so I took the chance.

"I'm Payton Mills," I said. "I'm new and—"

"Excuse me," the teacher's voice rang out. "This is homeroom, not a chat room. Enough talking, girls in the back."

The girl in front of me whipped her head back around.

"Sorry, Mrs. Galbreath," she said sweetly.

Great. My first attempt at conversation with someone who looked remotely cool, and I had to get her in trouble. Now she'd probably never speak to me again, and—

The girl smoothed her hair with her hand. And a note dropped onto my desk.

Don't let Mrs. Bad Breath get to you.
My sister had her and said she's evil.
Destroy this. —S

Mrs. Bad Breath. Heh. I smiled. If she really wanted nothing to do with me, she wouldn't have passed me a note, right? That was promising. I ripped the note up into teeny pieces. And I got ready to write her back. What should I say that would be cool, but not trying too hard?

Bad Breath! Ha! That's funny!

No, that was stupid.

I'm new and don't know anyone—

No, too desperate.

"Class, I need to step out for a moment," Mrs. Bad Breath announced. "Sit quietly and *behave yourselves*." She went out the door.

"Party time!" some guy called out.

Everyone started talking noisily.

"So." I cleared my throat to talk to the girl in front of me. But I didn't have a chance.

"Sydney!" Some other girl slid out of her chair and perched herself on the girl's desk. "What do you have next period?"

Suddenly there were girls surrounding the desk in front of me.

"Sydney, I looove your bag," another girl gushed. "It's so fabulous!"

"Syd!" some guy called out from the other side of the room. The girls all squealed and ran over there. I watched Sydney hug him.

I looked around for someone else to talk to, but the girl on my other side was talking to someone else. The guy on my other side had his head back. I think he was asleep. I leaned down and pretended to be engrossed in the contents of my tote.

My bag was stuffed full. I had a lunch box in there. Inside my lunch box was a paper bag full of food. That way, if everyone looked like they carried lunch boxes, I was good. But if everyone had paper bags, I'd junk the lunch box. I also had a few dollars in case it was cooler to buy hot lunch.

I also had stuff to decorate my locker with. I was seriously excited to finally have a locker of my own. I was ready for a serious locker makeover. Emma had made fun of me.

"What theme is your locker going to be?" I'd asked her.

"Theme?" Emma said. "How about gray and metal?"

"No," I said. "The inside. How are you going to decorate it?"

"A locker is a place for storage of serious academic materials," Emma replied. "Decorating it is a distraction."

She was crazy. My locker would be like my own room at school! My own little piece of the world! I was going to make it mine!

My locker theme was sheer genius. I'd thought of it at camp. The fashionista girls in my bunk would get these packages from their parents with new clothes in them. The shopping bags the clothes came in were so

cool—light blue, chocolate brown, black and white . . .
So I'd asked them if I could have them.

I'd cut up the cutest bags and was going to stick them
as a collage on my locker. I'd also brought:

- ☑ A light-up mirror with a pink boa frame
- ☑ A little pink holder for lip gloss, breath
  mints, and perfume spray
- ☑ A beaded curtain just like I had in my
  room at home, but mini-size
- ☑ Cute little magnets
- ☑ A picture of me and Emma on the first
  day of camp. I was going to leave some
  space for new pictures—hopefully ones
  of me and my new friends from school!

I also had some other stuff at home on standby—for
Emma's locker. Once I found out where her locker was
and snagged her combination, I was going to sneak in
and decorate it for her! I know she said she didn't want
to, but I was sure once she saw mine she would change
her mind.

". . . Max is looking hot!"

I looked up. Sydney and the other girls were back.

"Ew, he's all yours," Sydney said. "He's so sixth grade. I'm looking for something new, fresh, you know?"

I tried not to look obvious as I watched Sydney and the other girls talking. I wished I had a group of friends that would be all excited to see me. I thought back to my friends from my last school. They'd been my friends for a long time. But even then things felt like they were changing. I hadn't told anyone, but I didn't feel like I fit in.

I wondered if I could find a place to fit in here. I wondered if Sydney would be interested in a new, fresh friend. Like me.

"I can't believe I'm only in one of your classes, Syd," a girl sighed. "At least we have Science together. We can be partners!"

"Wait and see," Sydney said. "If Jazmine James is in there, I'm ditching you. Last year she was my science fair partner and totally annoying but did all the work. Easy A."

I wondered if I should tell her to keep an eye out for Emma. Emma had won our school science fair and would have gone all the way to state, but it was the same day as the state spelling bee, which was in our town. So my parents thought it would be easier to go to the bee. Even though we'd have gotten a free overnight at a hotel for the state science thing. With a pool and a hot tub . . .

"Bad Breath is coming!" someone hissed, and everyone scrambled back to their seats.

I fastened my tote bag and tried to memorize my locker number. 36—no wait, 306 something . . .

Clang! The school bell rang once. Okay! I was ready to get to my locker! I stood up and picked up my tote bag. Then I noticed I was the only one standing.

"It's just the warning bell," Sydney turned around and whispered to me.

Oh. I sat back down. But Sydney didn't turn back around. She looked me up and down.

"Let me see your skirt," she whispered.

I leaned out of my chair and showed her.

"Sweet," she said.

Sweet! She said it was sweet!

"Let me see your shoes," she said.

I held out my foot. I felt like I was being inspected. Would I pass? Would I fail? Sydney gave me a long look but didn't say anything. How could I keep the conversation going?

"I like your shirt—," I started to say, but—

Clang! Clang! Clang!

Everyone jumped up and went for the door. Sydney stood up and smoothed down her hair. Then she was swallowed up in a crowd of people. But before she disappeared, she turned around and waved at me.

I grinned. I picked up my tote bag and went to find my locker.

Emma

Four

HOMEROOM

I was the first person, alphabetically, in Homeroom 224, which put me in the first seat in the front row. The front row is my favorite place to sit. Preferably in the center seat, where I could focus on the teacher and the board. Plus, the teacher couldn't miss my hand waving to answer the questions, tee hee!

But this was just homeroom.

"Mills, Emma?"

"Here!" I raised my hand and smiled at the teacher. Sure, it was just homeroom. But it was always smart to make a good impression. The teacher didn't look up from his attendance sheet.

"Milton, Samuel?" he said.

Obviously not impressing the teacher, I lowered my hand and turned off my smile.

Then someone tapped my shoulder.

"What locker did you get?" a girl with reddish hair asked.

This was it! My first middle-school social interaction!

"Number 33639," I told her. "Isn't that cool? All the digits are divisible by three."

The girl gave me a weird look and turned to the girl on her right.

"Did you see Luke and Bryce in the hall?" Reddish-head said to the other girl.

"Yea. Sooo cute," the other girl responded. "Did you hear Luke and Raiya broke up at the pool? I'm so going after Luke."

"You wish," Reddish-head said. "He's so out of your league."

I tuned out. I missed Payton. Why wasn't she here in the seat behind me, like I'd planned? I stared ahead, and heard the voices of the class talking behind me. Were they talking about me? Were they saying, *What a snob; she won't even turn around?*

I could do it. I could do it. I forced myself to smile, and I slowly turned, this time to the left. A boy with brown hair was talking to the blond boy behind him. They ignored me. I glanced around, still grinning like an idiot. Nobody even acknowledged my presence. I whipped my head back around and faced front again.

Payton would tell me to chill out. I took a deep breath. I had more important things to do than chat right now, anyway. Like organize. I had my schedule now. Yay! I opened my backpack and took out my organizer and binder. I neatly placed my schedule on the desk beside them.

SCHEDULE Emma Mills		Grade 7	
Period	Subject	Teacher	Room
Homeroom	–	McGurty	224
1	Science	Perkins	113
2	Social Studies	Kay-Daniels	201
3	Lunch	–	Cafeteria
4	ELA (Advanced)	Burkle	266
5	PE/Wellness	Gregory	Gym 2
6	Study Hall	–	199
7	Spanish 2	Kane	218
8	Arts–Choir 2	Tellstone	222
9	Math (Advanced)	Cuyler	128

Science was first! I woo-hooed silently. That would start the day off with a bang. I placed my green folder (Science was always green) into the first slot of my case. I closed my eyes and pictured the science room. I was sure science in middle school would be in a real lab. Test tubes, measuring scales, safety goggles. So fun.

"Excuse me?" The boy turned from my left. Was he talking to me? I opened my eyes. He was! Oh, jeez. Did he think I was sleeping? That was embarrassing.

"You dropped your schedule," he said, handing me my paper.

Oh, I must have knocked it off my desk.

"Don't want to lose your schedule," he said. "That would be a nightmare; you'd have no clue where you were supposed to be."

"Oh, I'd know. I have it memorized," I blurted out.

"Already?" he said. "So then, what do you have fourth period? No peeking."

"English/Language Arts," I said, confidently. "Burkle, 266."

Oh. Burkle. As in Mrs. Burkle from the hallway outside the janitor's closet. Well, being in her class would give me a second chance to show how wrong her first impression of me was. I looked at the boy on my left.

"Next question?" I said.

"Seventh period," he challenged me.

"Spanish Two, Kane," I said.

"Man, you're good," he said. "How about third period?"

"Lunch," I said. "Cafeteria, of course."

"I have third-period lunch, too," he said. "What a joke."

I looked at the boy. I suddenly realized that he had nice green eyes. And that he was a boy.

When I got around boys, it was usually like my mouth had a mute button. I opened my mouth to say something else. I looked at his green eyes and . . . nothing came out. I felt my face turn as red as my folder. Red = Social Studies. I turned back to my binder and popped the red folder into slot two.

The boy started talking to someone on his other side.

Well, three sentences spoken out loud to a boy. That was practically my record!

Yellow folder, ELA . . . PE? Don't even think about that one. . . . Moving on to study hall . . . always good for doing extra-credit assignments. Then it hit me. What the green-eyed boy had said. Third-period lunch?

Third period was at 9:23. I had to eat lunch at 9:23 in the morning? Lunch?

The warning bell rang once. Oh no, only three minutes before homeroom ended. Lunch at 9:23 in the morning was almost as bad as Choir 2. I didn't sign up for Choir 1 or 2. This mathlete doesn't sing. I'd have to get Choir changed.

Next, Spanish. White. Blanco. La folder into el file. Finally, Math.

math math math math math math math math math math math math

I tenderly tucked my turquoise-blue folder into the last opening. Why turquoise? Because this summer at camp Payton had informed me that "To form separate identities, we needed to be seen as separate people."

"Payton," I'd said. "We're identical. Not Siamese. What are you talking about?"

"Signature colors," Payton said. "Mine is hot pink. What's yours?"

I knew Payton wouldn't drop the subject until I chose a stupid color. She got really stubborn about her crazy ideas. "Gray," I told her.

"You can't have gray!" she squealed. "It's so blah! So nothing!"

"It's the shade of my mechanical pencil," I said, holding up the pencil I was writing with.

"Just pick something else." She sighed.

"Fine," I said. I looked out the window of the cabin, where I'd spent most of the summer. It was a nice day. "Blue."

"Baby blue? Greenish-blue? Aquamarine?" she said. "Turquoise?"

"Sure, turquoise," I said. "Whatever. Now don't you have to go make Queen Ashlynn's bed or polish her toenails?"

Thinking about that reminded me of a secret I was hiding. Hiding inside my sneakers, to be accurate. Yesterday, I had . . . painted my toenails. I'd borrowed Payton's polish. My toes were now glittery turquoise. I know, I know. It seemed so shallow, so superficial. I couldn't believe I'd done it either. But for some reason my sparkly blue toes—in my, ahem, signature color— made me happy.

Clang! Clang! Clang! Homeroom was over. As I stuffed my organizer into my backpack, I noticed a small piece of bright pink paper in the bag.

You're a STAR!

Payton's handwriting. Too funny. When we were little, Payton had thought the song "Twinkle, twinkle" was about us. You know, "TWIN-kle, TWIN-kle, little stars." We sang, "TWIN-kle, TWIN-kle, little us," until we drove our parents crazy.

We have a video of us when we were little singing it. Payton was in a tutu, dancing and doing all the twinkly hand movements we'd learned in pre-K. Then there was me, singing off-key. At the end of the video, Payton says, "By Payton and Emma!" While she's curtsying, I give her a look as I announce: "No, it's by Wolfgang Amadeus Mozart."

Payton probably guessed I'd be stressed today, so she'd sent me some TWIN-kles on a stickum note.

I silently thanked my sister for the happy boost and the important reminder that I was a star. Then I raced out the doorway in a hurry to get to Room 113. A place where I would shine. Science class.

Payton

Five

ON THE WAY TO FIRST PERIOD

There it was. My own little slice of middle school.

Locker 33683.

I started walking up to it, but some skater guy got there first. And went up to my locker and—? Oh, wait. I double-checked the number in the envelope.

336**38.**

Wrong locker. I walked a little farther down the hall and found the right one. I checked my combination on my shoe and opened it on the first try. Yes!

I looked at my locker. Sure it was gray and boring and someone had written *I ♥ Jack* on it. But it had potential. I leaned down and opened my tote bag and got right to work. I only had five minutes, but I was going to make the most of it.

I started making a collage out of the cut-up fashion bags, sticking them on with sticky tack. I put up the magnets and the pictures and hung up the beady curtain. And last but not least—the mirror. Ta-da! I stood back to admire my work. I thought it looked pretty cute.

I looked in the mirror and checked my lip gloss. I definitely needed more lip gloss. I also seriously needed to brush my hair. Wait—why were there two of me in the mirror? I whipped my head around.

And Emma was standing behind me.

"You freaked me out!" I said, turning around. "I thought my mirror was reflecting double!"

"What the heck do you have in there?" Emma said. "I thought there was a light show going on in school."

"You did? Cool!" I said. "They're my special effects. Like them?"

I blinked the mirror lights on. Off. On.

"Stop! You're blinding me!" Emma said.

"Check out the rest of it!" I said. I opened it wide so she could see the beauty within. I looked at Emma's reaction. She looked a little stunned. Well, I couldn't blame her; my decorating job was pretty amazing, if I did say so myself. I couldn't believe I'd pulled it off so quickly either. She might even be a little jealous. Well, I'd do my best to decorate her locker later in the week.

"Well, this is great about your locker," Emma said.

"I'm glad you're so impressed with my style!" I said.

"Actually, I meant it's great because my locker is right next to yours," Emma said. "I'm number 33639! Right here!" Emma tapped the next locker over. "I was feeling like I'd never see you in school," she continued.

"Well, now we can catch up at our lockers!" I said happily. "What's new?

"Mainly, it was strange to be in homeroom without you. So thanks for the note with the star on it. It cheered me up, and—"

"Hey, are you two twins?" someone interrupted her. It was a girl who had a locker on the other side of Emma.

Emma looked annoyed at being interrupted.

"Emma, smile," I hissed.

I didn't want Emma to turn anyone off with that grouchy look. Especially since this girl might have friend potential, which would be convenient, since her locker was near us!

"Yeah, we're twins! Identical!" I said, smiling.

"Stand next to each other," she commanded.

It wasn't the first time this had happened. Emma and I stood next to each other.

"You're taller," the girl said to me. "And your eyes are a little bigger."

Yup, that was true.

"And your hair is a little darker," she pointed to Emma. "And your eyebrows aren't as bushy."

Hey! Wait a minute.

"Other than that, seriously identical," the girl said to herself, and walked away.

It was a weird twin thing, people wanting to compare the two of us. I mean, I obviously know I'm taller than Emma. And her hair *was* a little darker now, since she'd stayed in the cabin at camp all summer, out of the sun. But I'd never really thought about our eyebrows. Until now.

"My eyebrows are bushy?" I complained to Emma.

"Technically she didn't say bushy," Emma reassured me. "Just bushi*er*."

"Ergh, now I wish I had tweezers," I said, worriedly looking in my locker mirror. I blinked the lights on for a better look.

"I might have some tweezers in my science kit,"

Emma said, starting to unzip her backpack to check. Then she zipped it up again and gasped. "Oh, no! Science! I have to go! I need to get a good seat in Science!"

She was probably right. I should get to study hall to get a seat in the back. I quickly swiped on some lip gloss.

"Wait, I'll walk with you," I said. I started shoving books from my bag into my locker. I hadn't gotten to actually put any of my stuff away; I'd just been decorating.

"Payton, I really have to go," Emma said.

"Okay, okay, I'm almost ready," I said.

"Wow, twins," a girl said, a few lockers away.

"Big deal," a boy answered. "I know lots of twins."

"Yeah, but those two girls right there are seriously identical. I mean, Jake and Sam are identical, but Jake shaved his head for swim team, so at least you can tell them apart."

They shut their lockers and left.

I slammed my locker shut and looked at Emma.

"Want to shave your head?" I asked.

"Yes," she replied with a serious look. "Yes, I do."

We both busted out laughing. Then we started walking down the hall. Well, I walked. Emma ran. I hurried to keep up with her.

"So how was your homeroom?" I asked, a little out of breath from walking so fast. "Mine was pretty good. I met this girl. Well, kind of I did." I thought of how Sydney had at least turned around and smiled at me. "She looked really cool."

We walked down the hall together.

"Hey, there are those twins," we heard a girl say behind us. "One of them was in my homeroom."

"I think one of them was in my science fair once," her friend said. "I wonder if it's the same one."

"They're twins," said the first girl. "It doesn't matter. They're like the same person anyway."

Hello? We can hear you.

And we are definitely two Different—with a capital D—people, thank you very much.

Clang! The warning bell went off!

Two different people heading to two different classrooms!

"Here's my study hall," I said to Emma. "So . . . bye!"

I waved to Emma and went in to look for a promising seat. I found one almost all the way in the back off to the right and made myself comfortable.

Emma

Six

FIRST PERIOD

Clang! The warning bell went off.

Oh, no! *Don't freak out, don't freak out,* I told myself.

I freaked out.

I barely heard Payton call bye to me as she went into her classroom. I wasn't so lucky—my science class was on the other side of the building. Racing down the halls, weaving in and out of crowds, I got to room 113 just as three bells went off. Whew! I made it. I was out of breath, but at least science would calm me down. Once I found my seat, that is.

I scanned the front row. My usual favorite seat, front row center, was already taken. In it was that Jazmine person

I'd recognized at registration. I'd seen her outside of school at gifted enrichment programs, but I'd never talked to her. *I'll bet she'll be happy to know that at least one person in her class (moi!) can have fun scientific discussions at an advanced level. She'll probably want to be lab partners with me.*

I kept looking for a seat. There was Ahmad the robotics whiz. Another great potential partner. Looking . . . searching . . . the front desks were full. So were the ones in the second, third, fourth, and fifth rows . . . I stood there in the front of the room for an eternity until I saw it. An empty seat—in the back of the room. I walked to the back row and sat down. I'd never sat in a back row in my life.

I didn't like it.

I raised my hand and held it up. And up. And up. I realized the teacher couldn't see me behind all these people.

"Excuse me . . . um . . . Ms. Perkins?" I called out.

A small gray-haired woman stood behind a large teacher's desk. She turned and wrote on the board:

Dr. Perkins

"That's Doctor. Not Miss. Nor Mrs. And not Ms.," she said, glaring in my direction. Then she pointed at me. "You in the back, Miss . . ."

"Emma," I said meekly. I cleared my throat. "Emma Mills." I said that louder. There, that was more confident.

Soon Dr. Perkins would know the real me. Super Science Student.

"Yes, Miss Emma?" the teacher said.

"I'd really prefer a seat in the front," I said.

"Do you have vision problems?" Dr. Perkins asked.

"No, but . . ."

"Learning issues? Behavioral issues? A phobia of Albert Einstein?"

I followed her gaze and saw a large poster of Einstein behind me.

"An important lesson in science, Miss Mills," said Dr. Perkins, "is that sometimes there are variables you cannot control. In other words: Live with it."

Errgh. I slumped down in my seat. "Before we enter the wonderful world of science," Dr. Perkins said, "I'd like to congratulate one of our very own students for winning the state science fair. Jazmine James, would you please tell us about your award-winning project?"

"Of course," said Jazmine James from the front row center seat. *My* seat. Jazmine stood up and turned to face the rest of the class. I tried not to be too obvious as I checked out the competition.

"My project," Jazmine said, "was titled *Reducing our Environmental Footprint with Higher-Efficiency Enzyme Catalysts in Industrial Cleaning Compounds.*"

Some boy let out a loud yawn. Jazmine glared in his direction and kept talking about her experiment.

Fine. So she was definitely up there in the brains department. And that look she gave the yawner was certainly intimidating. A formidable opponent, this Jazmine James. I also couldn't help but notice that even Payton would be impressed: Jazmine not only sounded smart; she somehow looked organized and pulled together. Her tiny black braids were pulled back tightly in perfect rows into a ponytail. Her white shirt was as crisp as the papers in my organizer—well, before I dropped them. Her pencil skirt was as sharp as a, well, a pencil. Or as Payton would say, *Whoa. She is hot.*

Whatever. As everyone in the world of competitive academics knows, appearance doesn't matter. Preparation and performance do.

Like my performance at the state spelling bee, which had been scheduled the same day as the state science fair (or should I say the state science UNfair, since I couldn't compete in both). Anyway, at least I won the bee. Did I mention that? But I could have easily won the science fair, given the opportunity. Science was another one of my specialties.

I snapped back into the present when the class started clapping. I guessed Jazmine was finished showing off. I sat in the back and watched jealously. Nobody here knew I was a science whiz. Yet. I really had to show Dr. Perkins and this Jazmine James my stuff.

What would Einstein do? I tipped my head back and looked into his two-dimensional face. *Help me out here, Albert,* I pleaded silently. *Help me . . .*

"Ouch!" I'd leaned too far back. My chair skidded out from under me, and I crashed to the floor. Every face turned around to gawk at me. This was *so* not the attention I'd had in mind.

"Miss Mills?" Dr. Perkins said. "You were right. It appears you have a vestibular issue and need my careful monitoring to no further disrupt the class. You may pick yourself up and move your desk to the front."

Disrupt the class? Me? Did she say I have issues? Me?

"No . . . No . . ." I tried to protest that I was fine; I wouldn't need monitoring.

"Don't argue with me, young lady," Dr. Perkins interrupted. "You're walking on thin ice already. One more word and you'll get a conduct slip."

A conduct slip? But that was for the . . . BAD KIDS. I, Emma Mills, was being mistaken for a troublemaker for the second time today? First with Mrs. Burkle outside the janitor's closet, and now with Dr. Perkins in my science class. Could my first day in middle school get any worse?

"What's vestibular? Is that like a mental problem?" I heard someone say.

I felt my face turn bright red. I wanted to tell them it meant balance, but I wasn't allowed to say one more word.

I had no choice but to drag my entire desk-and-chair set toward the front of the room. *Screeech. Bump.* The desk was heavy and noisy, and I had to maneuver it around and through the rows of people to squeeze into a spot in front near the window. Everyone in the front row sighed and moved their desks to make room for me.

"Now that everybody is upright and quiet, let's begin," Dr. Perkins said. "We'll start with the Scientific Method."

I casually looked to my right—two seats down, center chair—at Jazmine James. She was paying rapt attention to Dr. Perkins. I straightened up, got my green notebook out, and did the same, through the entire class period.

When class ended, I gathered up my things and headed toward the door.

Jazmine James, a short olive-skinned boy with dark hair, and a very tall blond girl blocked my way.

"Emma, is it?" Jazmine smiled at me. See? I knew she'd recognize me from my accomplishments and be excited to talk to me.

"Emma, you poor thing," Jazmine said. "With your vestibular condition, do you need help getting to your next class so you don't tip over? Hector, take her backpack. Tess, hold the door open. Now, Emma, where's your next class? We can help you find it."

"No! That's okay!" I protested. "You misunderstood! I'm really—"

"She's so brave," said Tess, looking down at me and sighing.

"What class are you in next?" Hector asked, my backpack and his weighing him down.

"Social Studies, room 201," I said. "But I know where—"

"Room 201?" Jazmine said. "Well, that's too far for me. Hector or Tess, you'll have to take her. I need to be on time for Latin Two."

❀ 68 ❀

Latin 2? We didn't even have Latin 1 in my old school. *Darn! I'm behind already.*

"I have Social Studies with you!" Tess said, brightly. She took my backpack from Hector. "Let's go, Emma!"

I gave up. I followed Tess—and my backpack—out the door and off to Social Studies.

Seven

LUNCH

Okay. I'd gotten through Science, French, and Social Studies. But now was the true test of survival: lunch. I double-checked my tote bag to make sure I was ready.

Here was my plan:

I had packed a lunch bag inside a lunch box. I'd also brought lunch money. I was going to walk in to the lunchroom, casually look around, and then notice what more people were doing. Then I'd a) take out my lunch box and join a table, b) take my lunch bag out of the box, hide the box, and eat out of the bag, or c) keep my bag in a box inside my backpack, get out my money, and join the hot lunch line.

I took a deep breath and walked into the cafeteria. It was crazy, and I mean chaos. There were like thousands of people all excited to see each other and pushing around me to get to tables they'd apparently already planned out. The smells of pizza and hot dogs and whatever else was on the menu overwhelmed me. I felt dizzy.

Hot lunch? Lunch bag? That decision was suddenly the least of my worries. I stood there, not knowing what to do or where to go. Um . . . um . . .

"Patty!" I saw a hand waving over my way. "Patty, sit here!"

It was that girl Sydney from homeroom. Her hair still looked perfect. She was at a table full of girls who were all like *blah blah we have friends and an obviously cool lunch table*. Everyone at the table was either very pretty or dressed really nicely. Actually, both. I looked over my shoulder to see who the lucky Patty was who would get the empty seat that Sydney was pointing to.

"Patty, come ON!" Was it my imagination, or was Sydney talking to me? Patty, Payton . . . could be. I inched slowly toward their table. If they didn't mean me, I'd just smile and keep walking by. I'm sure they couldn't mean me. *La la la, just happening to walk near their table . . .*

And then, right when I got close, Sydney pointed to a chair.

"Sit," she commanded.

She was talking to me. She was definitely talking to me.

I went over and slowly sat down.

I kept my smile, but I was on guard. I mean, what if it was some kind of trick? Obviously, Sydney had enough friends, so why would she need me? Was it like in the movies: Let's play a joke on the unsuspecting new girl? I slowly pulled my chair up to the table.

"Everyone, this is Patty," Sydney said, pointing at me. "She's in my homeroom and she's new."

Everyone looked at me.

"Um, hi," I said. I smiled at everyone cautiously. "Actually, it's Payton."

"Patty's nickname is Payton," Sydney announced.

Everyone was like, "Hey." And then they turned back to talking and eating their lunches.

"Guess who my Spanish partner was today?" one girl said. "Bryce."

"Lucky!" some other girl said. "Hey, tell him to have another pool party this weekend. That last one was off the hook."

"I know, right?" Sydney said. "We were all like crazy. Remember when we did that thing in the pool?"

All the girls at the table started cracking up.

Well. Okay. I had nothing to contribute to this conversation. I decided to eat my lunch. Everyone at the table had packed, so I pulled out my lunch box. Then I opened my bag. No one seemed to notice or care about my lunch container. 'Cause no one was really looking at me. I started to eat my turkey wrap and watch the action.

And there was a lot of action. Most of it focused on Sydney. Two girls came by and complimented her. A guy came by and compared schedules with her. Some guys from the next table started shooting straw wrappers our way, and the girls at our table started squealing and shooting wrappers back.

"So, you're new?" the girl next to me asked.

I was chewing, so I nodded. By the time I'd swallowed, she'd turned to the girl on her other side. I opened up a little cup of peanut butter to eat with my apple.

"Payton!" Someone was saying my name. It was Sydney! "Payton, stand up!"

Uh-oh. This was it. I had to stand up and they were going to play some joke on me or something. What was it? Were they going to say, *Did you really think you could sit here?* and knock my chair over or something? I slowly stood up and accepted my fate.

"Turn around," Sydney said.

Oh, I bet I had a KICK ME sign on my back. Everyone was going to laugh at me.

"See?" Sydney said. "I told you."

"OMG, it's by TC Couture!" a girl with long black hair said. "Look at the label!"

Ohhh. They were talking about my Summer Slave skirt!

"How did you get that skirt, Payton?" someone asked.

Well. I cleaned out two gross shower stalls for it . . .

"Um—" I said.

"I want that skirt sooo bad." A girl with brown hair sighed. "They're not even in stores yet. How did you get it?"

Whoa, I didn't know this skirt wasn't even being *sold* yet.

"Oh"—I waved my hand, like it was nothing—"you know."

"Let me guess," a girl said. "Your cousin is a famous supermodel and she let you borrow it."

"Your dad is TC Couture's agent," someone else guessed. "Or wait. Your dad *is* TC!"

"Ohmigosh, is your dad TC?!" someone else squealed.

"No!" I blurted out. "He's not!"

"Maybe it's fake," the blonde with wavy hair said. "Is it fake?"

"No, it's real," Sydney said. "You can tell. And show them your shoes, Payton."

I held up a foot.

"So cute," someone else said. "What size are you?"

"Six," I told her.

"Ooh, me too!" the blonde said. "Well I'm a seven, but I could squeeze. Maybe I can borrow them? I have these pants that would be perfect for them!"

"Cashmere, leave the poor girl's closet alone," Sydney said. She looked at me. "That's Cashmere. She's a big clothes mooch."

The girl named Cashmere shrank back in her seat.

"And that's Quinn with the brown hair," Sydney said. "And Priya, and everyone else."

"Your shirt is so cute. I have the same one in green," said Quinn.

"Thanks." I smiled at her.

"We'll have to wear them on the same day," the girl said. "And Syd has a blue one!"

"Don't wear yours on Friday," Sydney said. "I have my outfit planned already. Payton, you can sit down. Isn't Payton's outfit so hot?"

Everyone complimented my outfit. I smiled and then sat back as they started talking about who was in whose classes.

And my moment was over. I tried to follow the conversation, but I didn't know anyone they were talking about. I just ate my lunch and pretended to know what was going on.

"You guys, poor Payton has no clue what we're talking about," Quinn said, smiling at me. "Let's clue her in."

"Okay, so Justin broke up with Aquilah," Cashmere said. "Which means he's free. So we're deciding if Sydney should go out with him."

"Everyone knows Justin has been in love with Sydney forever," someone said. "Everyone except Aquilah, anyway."

"Yes," Sydney said. "But I haven't decided yet. Cameron's looking hot too. I so can't decide. Or maybe Noah."

Must be nice to be able to choose. I wondered if everyone

had a boyfriend. I hadn't had one yet. In my old school there weren't any boys.

"Quinn's going out with Josh," Sydney said, as if she read my mind. "And Cashmere has a boyfriend from summer camp. Although we don't have proof he really exists."

"He just lives far away and isn't allowed to e-mail me," Cashmere protested. "He, um, has very strict parents. So Payton, what about you?"

I momentarily thought about making up a boyfriend too. Was that the right thing to say?

"Are you single right now?" Sydney asked.

"Yeah," I admitted.

"That's cool. Priya doesn't have a boyfriend, either," Sydney said.

Whew.

"But she doesn't want one. Do you?" Sydney asked.

I nodded. I did want a boyfriend. I'd just never really figured out how to get one.

"Ooh! We'll have to find Payton the perfect boy," Sydney said. "Just stay away from Cameron, Mac, Noah, and Justin until I decide. Oh, and Griffin, too."

"Okay," I said. This would be the year I'd get a boyfriend, I decided. The perfect boy. But not one of Sydney's boys.

"Let me see your schedule," Quinn said. I dug mine out and gave it to her. "Ooh, you're in my art class. Come sit next to me!"

"You're in my social studies class," Priya said, looking at my schedule and passing it on.

"You have last-period gym like Sydney," Cashmere said. "You guys are so lucky."

"Last-period gym is key," Sydney said. "You don't have to feel all sweaty and gross all day."

I nodded.

"So do you play soccer?" Sydney asked me.

"Um, no," I said.

"Oh, good, because Priya does, and she can never go anywhere with us until the season's over. It's a pain," Sydney said. "Do you want to go to the mall with us this weekend?"

"Me?" She was definitely looking at me. "Sure!"

"Cool," Sydney said. "Ask your parents if you can go. My older sister can drive us. We'll figure it out at lunch tomorrow."

Lunch tomorrow! Mall shopping with Sydney and her people! A search for my perfect boyfriend! Middle school was working!

Emma

Eight

DINNER

"Great!" Payton said at exactly the same time I said, "Okay."

We were answering Dad's question: "How was your first day at school?"

Dad, Mom, Payton, and I were at a Chinese restaurant to celebrate the first day of school. It was our annual back-to-school tradition. When I was five, our first day after kindergarten, I had glanced at the menu. And memorized it. When I told the server I wanted #72 with a side of #6, my parents realized I had a near-photographic memory. Normally, I love Chinese food, but I didn't feel much like eating tonight, especially after listening to Payton.

"Today was the best day," she was saying. "I sat with this girl Sydney and some other people at lunch and the rest of the day they showed me around and saved the best seats for me in class."

"You got good seats?" I groaned. Most of my classes had been so far away from each other that by the time I got to class I was stuck at a desk in a totally undesirable location. Like next to the heater, which clanked so I couldn't hear the Social Studies teacher. And next to some kid who snored and drooled in Math.

Adding annoyance to injury, in four—FOUR!— classes I was stuck watching Jazmine James in the front row, where I wanted to be. Where I deserved to be.

"You won't believe this," I told Mom and Dad. "I got to Math early by getting a pass out of Choir—"

Payton giggled.

"What?" I said, annoyed to be interrupted.

"YOU are in Choir?" she asked.

"I know, I know, I don't sing," I said.

"You CAN'T sing," Payton said.

"That's not the point," I said. "So I got to my Math classroom and it was empty. I went to my seat, front row center, and there was this little piece of paper on it. It said 'Reserved for Jazmine James.'"

I'd already told them about Jazmine James. And not only was her seat reserved, but the seats on either side of her had jackets holding spots for Jazmine's two cohorts, Hector Jordan and Tess Hamilton.

"This girl can reserve her seat?" my dad asked. "That doesn't seem fair."

"Jazmine James doesn't know the meaning of fair! She's evil," I said.

"Emma!" Mom was shocked. "That's a terrible thing to say. I know you had a bit of a difficult time today, but I'm sure everything will work itself out."

"Yea, Emma," said my sister loyally. "Once the smart clubs and after-school competitions start up, you'll find your people."

"Thanks, Payton," I said. "You're probably right."

That time couldn't come soon enough for me.

"I remember Mrs. James from one of Emma's events," my dad said, chewing on a spare rib. "Mr. James was very pleasant. We talked a bit about Jamaica, where he and his wife were raised. But Mrs. James wasn't particularly friendly, as I recall."

"Oh, Tom," my mother said. "She was probably just quiet. Not everyone introduces themselves to all the competition parents like you, dear."

That was true. Dad was always the life of the parent party at my competitions. He was friendly and talked to everyone. He always won salesperson of the month awards at the medical supply company where he worked.

Mom wrote articles for women's magazines. She had an office at home and wasn't as outgoing as Dad. Obviously I was more like Mom, personality-wise. Payton was like Dad. Our looks, however, were a combination of both. We were blond like Mom and had greenish-blue eyes like Dad.

"More tea?" A server came up to the table. She paused and said, "Twins?"

Dad said, "Yes, identical!" and started telling her how Emma was older, but Payton was taller.

"Dad!" I interrupted. Like the server really cared about our twin-ness?

"Do you twins like to pretend you're the other one and trick people?" the server asked.

Apparently, she cared.

"No!" Payton and I both said.

"They're very honest girls," my mother told her.

The server poured the tea and left.

"Girls, your father and I have to step out to the car for something," Mom said. "We'll be right back."

I wondered what they were doing. Well, they'd be back soon enough. I blew on my tea to cool it down.

"You know," Payton said, pouring sugar into her tea cup, "it was weird not hearing those twin questions all day. I mean, I thought we'd be in the same classes and have to explain ourselves over and over."

"Uh-huh," I agreed. It always happened when we went somewhere new, like camp. Today had been weird. But not good weird. I wouldn't have minded those questions, because it would have meant I actually got to see my sister in school. Not only was she not in my classes, but we kept missing each other at the lockers.

"It was good weird," Payton said.

Wait. Payton thought it was *good* weird?

"I felt like I could be, you know, just be myself for a change," Payton continued. "Not just one of the twins."

"Be yourself?" I snorted. "Sounds to me like you want to be Sydney's identical twin."

All Payton had talked about since school ended was Sydney this and Sydney that. It was like camp all over again; just substitute the name "Sydney" for "Ashlynn." Hopefully Payton wouldn't end up doing Sydney's laundry.

"I do NOT!" Payton said. "You're just jealous."

"Jealous?" I asked her. "Jealous of what?"

"Me and my new friends," Payton said.

"Please," I said. "Like I'd want to be one of those gossipy clothes clones."

"You don't even know who they are," Payton protested.

Well. Actually, I did know who they were. I'd heard people calling "Sydney!" enough in the halls to see who she was. Sydney was really pretty and was surrounded by other pretty people, some of whom I assumed were Payton's "new friends."

"I know who they are," I said. "They're people who believe they should be middle-school royalty. Falsely, I might add."

"What's that supposed to mean?" Payton challenged.

"Middle-school royalty should be those who excel in academics, not social life," I said. "Meaning people with superior IQs and grades."

"You mean like Jazmine James?" Payton shot back.

We both glared at each other, but just then Mom and Dad returned to the table.

"We're back!" Dad announced, handing us each an identical black box. "And we bring presents in honor of my wonderful twins' first day of middle school."

"Oooh! Presents!" Payton squealed.

I smiled too. Our conversation could wait. As much as I like a good debate, I also like a good present!

"Oh!" I said, pulling out a wide wristcuff. It was made of colored Lucite, with the letter *E* cut out of it.

"We had them specially personalized." Dad smiled.

"I love it!" Payton was already putting her *P* cuff around her wrist.

"We match!" I said happily. Matching bracelets would show off our twin bond, even while we were separated at school.

"Now people can tell us apart!" Payton said at the same time.

Okay. That too, I guess.

"They're so pretty," I said. "Thanks, Dad!" We both gave Dad a hug.

"My present next," Mom said, smiling. And she handed us each . . .

An iPhone! An iPhone!

"Ohmigosh!" Payton screamed, loud enough for people to look at us. "We have cell phones! I have my own cell phone! Thank you thank you thank you!"

We had been begging for cell phones for a long time. This was huge.

"It's a perfect back-to-school present!" Payton said.

"Wait," I said. "Isn't there some school rule against cell phones?"

Payton kicked me under the table. I shut up.

"The phones come with little doodads to personalize them," my mom said, handing us a little package of gem stickers in different colors.

"Give me all your pinks," Payton commanded me. "And I'll give you my turquoise ones."

"When I was your age," Mom said, "my best friend and I were split up into different classes. We'd write notes to each other and pass them in the halls between classes. I thought you two might like to stay in touch— the modern way."

"Text messages!" Payton and I hand-slapped over the table.

"Mom! Dad! You're the best!" Payton told them. "I love love love our presents!"

I checked out my phone. *Hmmm, there's a built-in calculator and time zone adapter*. I gave a silent *woo-hoo!* and scrolled through more features.

"I can't wait to show off my bracelet and cell phone to Sydney and my new friends at school tomorrow!" Payton said.

"I'm not surprised you're already making friends," Mom said to Payton. "You've always been so nice and popular."

"Nice doesn't always equal popular," I muttered.

"Hey!" said Payton. "I was nice *and* popular at our old school, Emma."

"So how is the old gang?" my mom asked her.

"Well . . . I e-mailed them, but I guess not so much since I got home from camp," Payton said. "It's been crazy busy, you know."

"Speaking of camp, what about Ashlynn and the Fashlynns?" I asked. "Have you heard from them?"

Payton frowned.

"No," she said. "But Ashlynn wasn't the *nice* popular type anyway, so who cares. Sydney and the girls are the popular *and* nice kind!" Payton brightened. "They saved me seats, and they were totally complimenting me all the time! And did I tell you I'm going shopping with them at the mall this weekend?"

"Wow," I said, sarcastically. "In seven hours you made FFBs!"

"It's BFFs." Payton rolled her eyes.

"Oh, darn, I'm not fluent in Popularese," I said. "I guess I'm too busy concentrating on important things."

"Having friends is important," said Payton. "And it's not so easy getting into the right group."

"Oh, how hard can it be to get into that group?" I retorted. "All you have to do is wear certain clothes and nod like a bobblehead at everything they say. You know, you could have been a little more creative with your choice of groups. I mean, you didn't go with the drama group, the sporty girls—okay, maybe not, you're not athletic—and obviously not the brains . . ."

"HEY!" Payton shouted, standing up.

"Girls, enough," my mother said.

But I couldn't stop. "There are hundreds of nice, normal people in our school, but nooo . . . you have to be in the 'kewl' clique."

Oops. That was loud. People at other tables were looking at us. The server came with the check. I calculated the tip for us as usual, Dad paid, and we walked out of the restaurant like a happy normal family that doesn't make scenes in public places.

Payton and I walked together through the parking lot.

"So, Emma. If it's so easy to be popular, then how come everyone isn't?" she said.

I wanted to say it was because not everyone wanted to be popular. But I knew that that wasn't exactly true. I knew that lots of people wished they were in the "in" group.

"Who cares? I mean, where does being popular get you in life?" I asked.

"Where? For one thing, the best seats in the classroom, unlike what *you* got stuck with," Payton said. "And also to the mall for a fun weekend, and to the best parties, and in the center of everything!"

"Whatever, Payton." I dismissed her.

"Well, where does being a brainiac get you?" Payton asked. "Sure, you get good grades, but you're stuck studying all the time."

"For starters, being a brainiac will get you into a good college—" I replied, but Payton cut me off.

"*If* you survive middle school first," Payton said. "You said it yourself. Your school day *stunk*. Mine was awesome."

"Girls!" my father said. "That's enough."

Payton climbed into the minivan and sat down in the second row. Instead of sitting next to her in my usual seat, I climbed into the third row by myself.

❀ 89 ❀

Payton didn't turn around.

I looked out the window as we drove out of the parking lot in silence.

BRRRZPP!

I jumped. What was that?

BRRRZPP! BRRRZPP!

My pocket was buzzing!

Oh! It was my cell phone vibrating! My first cell phone call! No, wait, my first cell phone text message!

I'm so kewl! Brainiacs drool! lol

That was one good thing about Payton. She never could stay mad.

I texted back:

u r so mature

Payton texted back.

I know! That's why I'm wearing TC Couture! T stands for TEEN!

I texted back:

& the C stands for Cheaply made since it broke & u had 2 go 2 the janitor's closet!

I heard Payton go, "AGH!" And then her face popped over the backseat.

"You *had* to bring that up?" she groaned. "I'm trying to block that whole tank-top thing out of my memory!"

"What was that, honey?" Mom said. "Did you say something?"

"Erp, no!" Payton called up front. "Nothing!" Her face disappeared again, and my cell phone vibrated.

ok the strap breakage thing was a bad start but it got better. hope sumthng good happened 2 u?

I thought back through my day. Well, there was that boy who quizzed me on my schedule. That would be something Payton would like to hear, I guess. I texted:

I talked to a boy in homeroom.

She responded:

u did?!!!! Was he cute???! appeared on my phone.

Yes & it was 3 whole sentences!

Go Emma! u rock!

"I'm so glad you're enjoying your cell phones, girls," Mom said cheerfully from the front seat. "I hear your fingers tapping."

"Text messaging is not unlimited," Dad warned. "Use it wisely."

At the exact same time, we slipped our phones into their cases. Then Payton's head popped back over the seat.

"One day of middle school day down!" she said cheerfully.

And 184 more to go. And that was just seventh grade.

Payton

Nine

LUNCH, THURSDAY

"Hi Payton! Love your shirt!"

"Thanks!" I said, smiling back at the girl passing me in the hall. I was stopping at my locker to drop off some books before I headed to lunch. I walked right up to my locker. I didn't even have to remember the number anymore—Sydney had written **Luv ya!** ♥ on the front in dry-erase marker. It was smudgy, but I was leaving it on there.

I opened my locker on the first try. Yesterday had been my second day of middle school success, and it looked like today would be lucky too. I clicked the lights in my locker mirror. I looked pretty good today, I thought. I was wearing:

- ☑ A yellow baby doll top
  (Summer Slave couture)
- ☑ Jeans (also Summer Slave) rolled up
- ☑ Headband with a yellow and gray design on it
  (Summer Slave)
- ☑ Shoes with a little bit of platform heel
  (Yeah, Summer Slave)
- ☑ Bracelet with the *P* on it (mine!)

I put on lip gloss and smiled, satisfied. I'd done a pretty good job with the eyebrow tweezing the other night. It was painful, and my right eye had been swollen for an hour, but now my eyebrows were as thin as Emma's.

I dug around for my lunch bag behind my books. Emma was bugging me about my locker being disorganized. Like her locker was so amazing. She still hadn't decorated it at all—and she wouldn't even give me her locker combination. She said I'd ruin her system. I was determined to get in there somehow and redecorate. I had big plans.

My cell phone vibrated with a text message. I pulled it out and took a second to admire it. I'd decorated it with pink and silver sparkle sequins in a cute pattern.

When do u want 2 meet at our lockers? Me

Hmm. When could I meet Emma at our lockers? I was supposed to meet Sydney at hers before gym, stop by Quinn's after lunch, and—

"Payton, Payton." It was a girl I recognized from science class. "Are you mad at me?"

"What?" I barely knew her. "Am I mad at you? Um, no . . . ?"

"Oh, good, because you didn't say hi to me in the hall before," she said. "So I thought maybe you were mad at me! I was like, 'Oh no! What if Sydney is mad at me and she told you guys to blow me off?'"

Oh, I understood. She'd seen Emma in the hall, and of course Emma hadn't said hi because she didn't know her.

"That wasn't me before; that was my twin—," I started to explain, but she was heading off to her next class.

I grabbed my stuff for lunch. A bunch of people said hi to me. Everyone noticed Sydney, of course, and thanks to her, now people were noticing me. In my old school, everyone knew me. But they had known me and Emma—the twins. This school was so huge—not everyone even knew I had a twin!

Oh! My twin! I'd forgotten to text Emma back. I pulled out my phone and started to, but another text came in—

P! we r waiting at lunch 4 u!

It was Sydney. I'd better hurry.

I walked into the cafeteria, waving at a couple of people as I went by. Then I headed straight for our lunch table. I'd learned to pack lunch—never buy except on pizza-delivered-in day. And never bring in a thermos of soup, either. I'd had to deal with Sydney and Cashmere making fun of my slurping.

"Oh, good, you're here," Sydney said. "We're planning when to go shopping."

"Yay, shopping," I said, sitting down. Just then my phone rang. It was Emma.

"That's your ringtone, Payton?" Sydney said. "That song is so over."

"Um, yeah, I know," I said. "I was planning to change it, but I've been so busy—"

"I'll download you something that's more you," Sydney said, taking my phone and hitting Off. Guess I wasn't taking that call.

"Payton, I love your headband," Quinn said. "It looks really pretty with your hair."

"Thanks," I said, and smiled at her.

"I just love that store," Sydney said.

"Oh, me too," I said knowingly. "Like when you walk in, it's so . . . you know."

"Exactly," Sydney said. "Totally."

Whew. I had no clue where Ashlynn had gotten this headband.

"Sydney, I love your shoes," I said. "So cute."

"I know, right?" Sydney said. "I'm thinking about getting them in silver, too, and—hey!"

A balled-up napkin landed right in front of her.

"You guys!" Sydney turned around and gave a dirty look to the guys at the table behind us who threw it at her. "They are so immature. Those are the football players, Payton."

"But so hot," Cashmere sighed. "I mean, look at Ox's muscles. We are so going to win the football game next week with him as quarterback."

"He's hot." I nodded with everyone and looked at the guy with the biggest muscles; I assumed he was the guy you'd call Ox. He looked back at me, so I gave him a flirty smile. He frowned and turned his back to me.

Ooookay. That was mildly embarrassing. I hadn't really gotten the flirty-smile-to-the-guys thing down yet. I had gotten the smiling-and-nodding-with-the-girls thing down, though, and I contributed smiling and nodding to my table's debate about what to wear the next day. Coordinating outfits with friends? So kewl.

I unwrapped my turkey wrap and pulled out the lettuce before I ate it. Cashmere had been eating a salad the day before, and Sydney had made her laugh three times so we could all see the lettuce stuck in her teeth before she clued her in. I was taking no chances.

"I need new shoes," Sydney said. "Payton can help me pick them out. Doesn't Payton have the best shoes?"

"I guess," Cashmere said. Then her eyes narrowed as she looked at me. "How come you always buy your shoes too big on you, though, Payton?"

Uh. I didn't really have an answer to that, since I'd never actually bought any of my shoes. Cashmere was looking at me expectantly. Er. Uh.

My cell went off.

"I gotta take that," I said, relieved.

"Is that your sister calling you or texting you again?" Sydney groaned. "I mean, I know you're twins, but she acts like you're Siamese attached to each other or something."

She reached over and hit the power off button again. Um, this was *my* phone? I tossed it in my backpack. I'd scroll through "missed calls" later.

"I can't believe you have an identical twin," Quinn said. "That's so weird."

"You know what's weird is how different they are," Cashmere said. "Wasn't your sister wearing sweatpants yesterday?"

"Um, yeah," I sighed. "She was."

"It must be a little embarrassing," Sydney said, as she polished her apple. "To have someone who looks like you walking around with such a desperate fashion sense. What if people think she's you?"

Sydney recoiled in horror.

I wanted to defend Emma, but in a way Sydney was right. Emma could be embarrassing. But that didn't mean Sydney had to say that. Nobody should talk about my sister that way! I opened my mouth to defend Emma.

But then I closed it. What was I supposed to say? I mean, they were right. How many times had I tried, tried sooo hard, to get Emma to wear something cute? I mean, sweats? Not cute sweats—baggy, don't fit, don't care sweats. Once she even wore them with black flats. Now, *that* was totally embarrassing. What if people *had* thought that was me? I opened my mouth to agree with Sydney.

Then I shut it. Emma was my twin, after all! I would stick up for her!

I opened my mouth to defend Emma again. But not soon enough.

"So, like, before you were born do you think you sucked up all the genes for fashion, leaving her with none?" Sydney said. "And all the genes for a social life. I mean, no offense or anything, but does she even have any friends?"

Clang! Clang!

The bell rang before I could say anything. I hadn't finished my lunch, but oh well. I'd lost my appetite, anyway.

Emma

Ten

LUNCH, FRIDAY

"Emma, it's so wonderful to see you looking well-balanced," Jazmine James said. "And your chair is staying upright too."

"Gee, thanks," I said sarcastically. "I'm really starting to get this equilibrium thing down."

It was third-period lunch, and I was seated across from Jazmine James. As usual Hector and Tess were with her.

What was not usual was me actually eating lunch in the cafeteria. On the first day of school I'd walked into the crowded cafeteria, holding my lunch bag. I'd recognized only three faces: Jazmine, Hector, and Tess. They were sitting at a four-person table. I slowed down when I got near them.

"So sorry, this seat's saved," Jazmine said, sliding her backpack onto the empty seat. I sped back up and kept walking, out of the cafeteria, down the hall, and to the school library.

I was not happy. Don't get me wrong. I L-O-V-E the library. Books! Reference materials! Internet access! What's not to love? It's just that being forced to hide out there during lunch was a little embarrassing. And inconvenient.

The library media specialist (aka the librarian) greeted me with a friendly smile as I gave her my honors pass. I'd been issued the honors pass along with my class schedule—a privilege for top students. It meant I was eligible for special field trips and certain clubs, and I was allowed to go to the library at any time, as long as I wasn't skipping class.

I wasn't skipping class, but I felt guilty. I wasn't there to study or to read. I found a study desk in the back and oh-so-inconspicuously ate my lunch. And picked up every crumb afterward to leave no evidence of my breaking the rule about eating in the library.

Grr. Jazmine James. I'd never broken a school rule

in my entire life, and thanks to her I'd done it on the first day of middle school.

On the second and third days I hadn't bothered to slow down as I walked through the cafeteria. Unfortunately, it was the only direct way to the library, and I didn't want to get caught roaming the halls. But even zooming through the lunchroom, I could see Jazmine's table. And I noticed that there was always an empty seat.

Today was different. Jazmine surprised me by stopping me as I walked by.

"Tess's mother?" Jazmine said. "She met your father at the hospital where she's a doctor, right? He sold her some medical apparatus. He mentioned you've been having a rough time so far at school. So Tess's mom told us to invite you to sit with us at lunch."

I cursed my father in my head.

"Thanks, but I'm doing fine!" I said brightly.

Total. Lie. My classes so far had been blah. The teachers were doing basic review to make sure everyone got off to a good start. So even though teachers called on me sometimes, the questions were easy. I'd had no opportunity to be math-mazing or science-sational.

"My dad must have been talking about my twin

sister, Payton," I continued babbling to Jazmine. "But fine. Sure. I'll eat lunch with you. To make Tess's mom happy."

Now I had the opportunity to eat at Jazmine James's lunch table out of pity. Yee-ha. Well, it couldn't be worse than sneaking food into the library. I was so glad it was Friday. I needed the weekend to figure out how to get myself back on track. My first week of middle school had been an unqualified disaster.

I opened up my turkey wrap.

"Hi, Jazmine!" A girl walked by our table.

Jazmine rolled her eyes.

"Courtney Jones," she said. "She's the one whose hamster escaped at the science fair last year. She was all crying about her poor pet."

"That's terrible!" I said.

"No, it was excellent," Jazmine laughed. "She got last place, because how do you do hamsters going through a maze without a hamster?"

Harsh.

"She found the hamster later," Tess reassured me.

"Did you know Jazmine has the highest IQ in the history of this school?" Hector suddenly announced.

"Hecky!" Jazmine slapped his arm playfully. "Emma

doesn't want to hear about that! Let's talk about your solo in the youth symphony."

"Hector plays seven instruments," Tess shared. "He's a music prodigy."

"He's also a computer whiz," Jazmine added. "Which is how he hacked into the school database and got everyone's IQ scores."

"The program wasn't even protected, and the password was obvious," Hector said. "That's not hacking. That's practically advertising to the public."

"Don't tell me mine!" squealed Tess. "I don't even want to know!"

I chewed my turkey wrap and swallowed hard. If I kept eating, maybe nobody would expect me to talk.

"Okay, I won't tell you, Tess," Hector said. "Even though it's practically the same as mine."

"Impressive," Jazmine cooed.

Then Hector looked at me. He had beady eyes.

"The data was updated last year, so your IQ score wasn't entered, Emma," Hector said. "What is your IQ?"

Everyone looked at me. Jazmine's eyes narrowed.

"I don't know," I said, my eyes down. "My parents won't let me find out."

"Don't you need to put it in your applications for the gifted programs and challenge competitions?" Jazmine asked me. She had finally recognized my name and told Hector and Tess about my spelling-bee win.

"Actually, I am dying to know," I admitted. "My parents have this thing about not telling. Because I have an identical twin sister, and they don't want us to compare."

"It's so cool you have an identical twin," said Tess.

"It must be hard to go up against your own sister in competitions," Hector said.

"Payton's not really into competitions," I told them.

"Ohhh," Jazmine said knowingly. "Is Payton, you know, slow?"

She leaned closer to me.

"Before you were born, were you the twin who sucked up most of the brain cells, leaving the other twin without a chance?" (Was that true? Could that happen?)

"What?!" I said. "NO!" (I'd have to research it on the *Journal of Medicine*'s website. Maybe Jazmine had scientific knowledge about twins that I'd missed. Oooh, if it was true—poor Payton.)

"It must be a little embarrassing," Jazmine went on, "to have someone who looks like you walking around with inferior intelligence. She could ruin your academic reputation. What if she answers a question and people think she's you?"

Jazmine recoiled in horror.

I started to defend my poor, brain-deficient twin, but in a way Jazmine was right. Payton could be embarrassing.

"Well, no sense worrying until the competitions start up," Jazmine said. "This year I'm going for the triple: science fair, spelling bee, *and* mathletics."

Who does Jazmine think she is? I thought. Then I slumped. Yeah, it was possible the trophies would be hers. The front row center seat? Hers. The whole middle school seemed to belong to Jazmine James.

I sighed. And chewed.

"Hey!" I heard a voice call from the next table. "Girl genius!"

Jazmine turned around. Her dark ponytail swung gracefully.

"Yes?" she said. "Do I know you?"

"No," a boy said. "I'm talking to her."

He pointed at me. Jazmine turned around in a huff and glared at me.

It was the boy from homeroom.

"What did I tell you?" he called over. "Third-period lunch is a joke!"

"You were right!" I called back, pleased that he remembered me. And that he called me a genius. In front of Jazmine James.

"How do you know Nick?" Tess asked. "I read his articles in the sixth-grade paper last year. They were good. He seems nice."

"Whatever, he's totally not in our league," Jazmine said dismissively. "I've never even seen him in a competition. Nice doesn't equal brains."

I looked at Jazmine. Obviously not.

"So, Emma, what instrument do you play?" Jazmine asked, changing the subject. "I'm first-chair viola. Hector's first-chair violin. Tess is first-chair cello."

I froze in my seat. I couldn't exactly say I was first chair in Choir, since we all stood up to sing. Not to mention, with *my* voice I'd probably be closer to last chair.

"Um . . . I'm taking private lessons this year," I improvised.

Okay, I lied. I panicked. How was I supposed to admit to these musical geniuses that I had no musical talent whatsoever? I know, I know. There's always this thinking that the smartest kids are musical whizzes. That just isn't me.

"What instrument do you play?" asked Tess.

"With whom do you study?" asked Hector.

I took a quick look at the clock. I "accidentally" dropped my lunch bag and fumbled under the table for it.

"She must be really good if she gets out of Orchestra for privates," I heard Tess say.

I stayed under the table. One . . . two . . . three . . . *Cl-cl-clang!*

"Oh! The bell!" I popped my head back up over the table. "Time to go!"

"Emma, tell us all about your music next week at lunch," Jazmine said.

Another lunch? With this group? *Bluh.* I'd thought that having a place to sit in the cafeteria would make me happier. But proving myself to Jazmine and her cohorts just made me feel sick to my stomach.

Payton

Eleven

LUNCH, FRIDAY

Oh, shoot.

I'd forgotten my lunch. On our kitchen counter was a brown bag containing a peanut butter and jelly sandwich, an apple, a granola bar, and a brownie.

Agh. I had two choices: Buy lunch or starve. The first choice seemed like the obvious one, but it really wasn't.

"Hot lunch is disgusting," Sydney had said. "And the soup and sandwich option is even grosser. Don't *ever* buy."

I walked into the cafeteria and could feel my stomach growling. I'd just go ahead and buy a little something; it really was no big deal. I went up to stand in line.

The line was seriously long. I leaned against the railing as I waited. I had on a pair of Summer Slave shoes that were totally adorable—wedge heels with teeny polka dots on them. The polka dots were teeny, but the heels weren't. They were pretty high.

"Hi, Payton!" the girl in front of me said. "I'm in your gym class! I was on your team when we played volleyball yesterday; remember me?"

"Yeah," I said, looking down. I remembered her, because Sydney had made fun of the way she served the ball. She seriously had looked like a chicken, but I felt bad now for laughing. "Hi."

"Isn't Sydney awesome at volleyball?" she said as I picked up a tray and looked at the lunch choices. "I think she was impressed with my overhand."

I nodded but didn't look at her.

"The burrito isn't bad," the girl said. "You should get that."

"Okay, thanks," I said. I put a burrito wrapped in aluminum foil on my tray. I put an orange and a cookie on and slid my tray down. I paid for my food and walked toward my lunch table.

"Hi, guys!" I said, sitting down in my usual seat between Quinn and Sydney.

❀ 111 ❀

"Did you buy lunch?" Quinn said, as I sat down next to her. "That's brave."

"I forgot my lunch," I said, unwrapping the burrito. "No biggie."

"Maybe no biggie for you, but how about for those of us who have to smell it?" Sydney said. "Ew, that's disgusting."

"What is in that thing?" Cashmere asked, leaning across the table. "It looks like poo."

"I guess it's beans," I said, looking at it closely.

"Well, it's grossing me out," Sydney said.

Alrighty. I wrapped the burrito back up in foil and pushed it off to the side of my tray. I started peeling the orange.

"So!" I said, brightly. "Aren't Sydney's earrings the cutest?"

"I know, right?" Sydney said. "Hey, we're making a plan for the mall. You're coming, right? You obviously need some new clothes."

"I'll be there," I said. *Wait.* "Um, why do I need some new clothes?"

"You're wearing your pink shirt again," Cashmere said. "That's the second time."

"Um," I said, "I guess. But this time I'm wearing it

with *this* jacket. So it's practically a new shirt, right?"

"And you wore the same jeans twice already," Sydney said. "Payton, Payton. We expect more of you."

I shifted uncomfortably in my seat. More? What more did they expect? I couldn't meet much higher expectations, especially because I was running out of Summer Slave clothes I hadn't worn yet. I'd thought I could mix and match pieces from those five outfits I'd slaved for. Uh-oh.

"We'll go crazy shopping this weekend," Cashmere said. "Bring your credit card!"

I didn't have a credit card. I didn't have any cash, either. I'd get my allowance on Saturday, which meant I'd have about . . . ten dollars to spend. I could get new . . . socks.

This was not good.

"Payton's slipping," Sydney said, shaking her head. "Clothes, a smelly burrito . . ."

BRRRZPP!

Saved!

"My cell! I have to take this," I said.

"Is that your twin sister texting you *again*?" Sydney said. "Hey, I have a great idea. We can bring your sister to the mall too. You can buy her some new clothes."

"You know what, she's not really into clothes," I said.

"Duh, obviously," Sydney said. "Let me see your phone."

She talked as she texted: "Emma. Don't text me again until you've had a makeover."

"You're not really typing that, are you?" I said.

Sydney ignored me.

"You are ruining my image with your hideous clothes," she said out loud as she typed. "And brush your hair."

"Okay, wait," I said. "You're not really texting that to my sister, are you?"

I mean, okay, Emma might not be into clothes. But I didn't want to crush her feelings or anything.

"Payton," Sydney said, smiling at me. "It's just a joke. Chill."

"Oh." I breathed a sigh of relief. "I thought you were seriously sending that text."

"I'm just trying to do you a favor," Sydney said. "You know as well as I do that your sister's embarrassing."

"SYDNEY! STOP!" I said. Loudly. Too loudly. People from other tables turned around and looked at us.

Uh.

"Payton, ohmigosh. Now *you're* embarrassing *us*," Sydney said.

She slid my phone back to me across the table.

"I was only trying to do you a favor," Sydney said. "But I don't appreciate being yelled at."

Uh. Oh.

I took my phone and looked at everyone. Quinn and Priya were looking down at the table. Cashmere was looking at . . . my lunch tray?

"Ewwww!" Cashmere shrieked, pointing. "Payton's burrito is oozing all over!"

I looked down. Oh. Ew.

I saw Sydney looking at me in disgust. I needed to get out of there.

"I think I'll just throw this in the garbage," I stammered, and picked up my tray. And that's when I felt it. I forgot I was wearing Summer Slave platform heel shoes. I wobbled. And I fell forward, and—

"Payton! Look out!" Quinn screamed.

My lunch tray was sliding out of my hands! I watched in horror as my oozy burrito slid farther and farther toward . . .

Sydney! Noooo!!! My oozy burrito was sliding toward Sydney! Quinn and Cashmere were looking at me like, *ACK!*

I had only a second to act. I regained my balance and yanked the lunch tray back and—

Whew! The burrito slid back, away from Sydney! Whew! I steadied myself on my shoes.

Except that the burrito slid the other direction and flew over my head and behind me.

"What the—?!!" I heard someone yell.

I turned around and saw the guy called Ox jumping up. With a big brown splotch on his shirt.

"Ewww!" Cashmere said. "Gross!"

Everyone was looking at me. Well, they were looking at Ox, who was pointing at me, so then they were looking at me.

"I—uh," I stammered. "I gotta go."

I grabbed my tote bag. And was out of there.

Emma

Twelve

PE, FRIDAY

BRRRZPP! BRRRZPP!

My cell phone would not stop buzzing. I ignored it
and watched everyone else in my class whack the volleyball across the net. The gym, like everything in this school,
was humongous. There were about six different PE classes
going on at the same time.

"Temporary carpalmyalgia," I had told my
PE teacher. "That's pain in the hands and wrists."
Mr. Gregory looked at me for a minute, then told me to
sit on the bleachers.

Hee.

Knowing the Latin derivatives of words really helped

make up great excuses. I mean, PE? When would I ever need those skills in my future career?

BRRRZPP! BRRRZPP!

Plus, I am a klutz.

BRRRZPP! BRRRZPP!

I ignored my cell. The last two times I had checked my text messages, they'd been insults. From Payton. Things like, "You're ruining my life!" and "Get a make-over!"

If that was her idea of a joke, it wasn't funny. And if she was serious? I would not take this lightly. I was starting to get all worked up, so I went to my happy place: mental math.

I tried to do square roots in my head, but it was impossible to calculate with volleyballs flying, whistles blowing, people cheering, and other people booing. Plus, that gym smell—combination of floor wax and BO-was overpowering my cognitive abilities.

BRRRZPP! BRRRZPP! I gave up and pulled out my cell phone, turning so Mr. Gregory couldn't see. I had enough problems without Payton turning into an evil twin. Without reading my messages, I texted Payton back.

im busy. and u r a snob.

BRRRZPP! BRRRZPP! She texted back.

K EmergenC!!!!

Well, I really wasn't that busy warming the bleachers. Might as well go see what the drama queen wanted. I texted back to meet me at our lockers.

K but hurry!!! ☹

"Mr. Gregory!" I called out, and hopped off the bleachers. "I need to run my achy hands under warm water so my condition doesn't get aggravated."

He waved me off to go.

I took the hall pass in my achy (not really, hee) hand, grabbed my bag, and left the gym. I didn't need to change or anything; my PE clothes were my regular clothes: sweats, T-shirt, and sneakers.

When I got to our lockers, I saw Payton. Well, part of Payton. Her head was in her locker.

"Looking for something?" I asked.

Payton turned around.

Whoa. She looked awful. Was she crying? She was.

"I can't do this!" she wailed. "What should I do? I don't know what to do!"

"Um," I said, stalling for time. I'd never seen Payton like this. She was getting hysterical. I looked up and down the hallway. It was empty now, but what if someone came out? I knew Payton wouldn't want people to see her like this. We needed somewhere private.

The girls' bathroom? No, people were always in there. Aha! I knew! I ripped Payton's mirror off the locker wall and grabbed my sister's hand before she could say anything.

"Come on," I said, and guided her to the janitor's closet.

Yes. The site of Emergency #1: The Tank-Top Strap Attack Incident.

The door was unlocked, so I dragged Payton inside and shut the door behind us.

"Ewww," we both said as the smell hit us. I heard a little spritzy sound, and suddenly the closet smelled like flowers. I felt for the mirror and turned on the light. Now we could see.

The janitor must have taken his mop and bucket with him. There was only an empty space. I looked around. Gray walls. No green or white or geckos. An oasis in the middle of middle school.

"Well, this place isn't *so* bad," I said out loud.

I saw Payton put a little fragrance spray back in her tote bag.

"Good," she sniffed. "Because I'm never coming out. I can never show my face in school again."

Her face crumpled and she started crying again.

"Payton, calm down," I said. "What happened?"

"It was at lunch," Payton wailed. "First, Sydney was pretending to send fake text messages on my cell phone—"

"You mean the 'You are so hideous' messages?" I said. "That was Sydney?"

"You got those?" Payton's eyes got wide. "She sent them for real?"

"Yeah, I thought you sent them," I said.

"Oh, no! If she sent mean messages to you, and she doesn't even know you . . . what is she going to do to me?" Payton wailed. "I'm doomed! Sydney's going to turn everyone against me! Why did I forget to bring my stupid lunch today?!"

"Just tell me what happened," I said.

"She got mad! I tripped! It flew! And . . ."

She took a deep breath.

"I OOZED OX!" Then she dissolved into more tears.

Oh. Kay. Clearly my twin sister had lost her mind.

"Payton, you're right," I said. "You're a mess. You can't go out there in this condition."

I had a thought. A crazy thought.

CLANG! It was the warning bell.

No more time to think. Just do.

"Quick," I said. "Switch clothes with me."

"What?" Payton said.

"Don't talk; just move," I said. "Give me your clothes."

I turned my back to Payton and pulled my sweatshirt over my head. Then I kicked off my sneakers and started stepping out of my sweats.

"Emma, I told you! It was Sydney who said that about your outfit," Payton protested. "I don't really care what you're wearing. At least, anymore."

"This isn't about me," I said. "It's about you."

Seeing my sister so upset made me feel bad. But it was more than that. I had stopped feeling sorry for myself and started thinking about someone else for a change.

"Hurry up and change!" I insisted. "Put on my clothes! And give me yours! I'll go out there as you.

Hanging out with your friends is all about faking confidence? I can do confident."

It was true. Before middle school started, I *was* confident and self-assured. Who didn't crack under pressure at the spelling bee sudden-death round? Me! Emma Mills!

"You're going to pretend to be me?" Payton was starting to catch on.

"Yes! I can be Payton with her head held up high," I told her. *Me, "Payton" Mills!* "Well, for one afternoon anyway. That's just four periods."

Payton thought for a moment. I held up the mirror so she could see what she looked like.

"Let's do it," Payton said.

Payton and I traded outfits. I put on jeans and a pink shirt with some strappy things. I slipped on her shoes and . . . holy moly. How did a person walk in these things? Ve-e-ery carefully, I guess. Payton slipped into my sweats, still snuffling.

This felt weird.

"Wait!" Payton said. She whipped out a makeup kit. *AGH!*

Payton powdered some stuff on my face, glossed my lips, and smoothed down my hair.

"There," she said. "Now you could be me."

"I *am* you," I said, confidently. "I am Payton!"

I took a sanitizing wipe from my bag and gave it to Payton, who wiped the tears off her face. All of her makeup came off with it.

There, the natural look.

"And you're going to be me!" I told her. "Look, here's my schedule. Just lay low in study hall, and give a note to Señora Kane claiming laryngitis. And Choir? You can't do worse than me in Choir anyway. Last period is Math. Don't even try it. Just go to the nurse. I'll meet you at our lockers for the bus."

"Thanks, Emma," said Payton. I opened the closet door to leave. I had Payton's schedule memorized, so I knew where I was going.

"Emma!" Payton called. "Switch bags! And don't forget! Our bracelets!"

We quickly slipped off the *P* and *E* and put them on each others' wrists.

"Promise you won't do anything too weird?" Payton said, sniffling.

"Promise you won't let any snobby people use my iPhone?" I asked.

"Promise to try to make Sydney not hate me so my

middle-school life isn't completely shattered so you and I won't *both* be middle-school outcasts?"

I was smart. I would figure out how to do all of that. How hard could it be to be Payton anyway? I'd just say "yeesh" a lot.

"Yes, yes," I said, impatiently. "Wait, I'm not an outcast! But no time for that. Now, you promise to hurry up so I'm not marked as late for study hall?"

Payton nodded and held out her hand. I reached out, and we linked our pinkies.

"TWIN-ky swear," we both said.

A TWIN-ky swear was like a pinky swear, only bigger. You could never, ever break a TWIN-ky swear.

"Let's do it," Payton said, taking a deep breath. She opened the door and slipped out first. Then it was my turn.

I stepped out into the hallway.

"There are those twins," said a girl to her friend. "One of them is in my study hall."

Payton and I glanced nervously at each other.

"The one in the sweats," she continued, pointing at Payton as she walked past us.

Excellent! That girl was in my study hall. I gave Payton a confident look. "Let's do it!"

Clang!

We bolted. Payton headed left to my study hall. And I went to the right, to Payton's English class. Oops. It was Mrs. Burkle. The one teacher Payton and I both had. I hoped she wouldn't notice I was back. Nah, she wouldn't be able to tell it was me. I'd slip in so nobody would notice.

I made it five steps before the platform shoes got me. I wobbled precariously and nearly fell over. I managed to grab onto Mrs. Burkle's desk and keep my balance.

"You! In the too-high-for-school shoes! Weren't you in my earlier class?" Mrs. Burkle's booming voice said loudly. Apparently middle school teachers had so many students to keep track of they didn't even notice identical twins. Until one of them practically fell on their face right in front of them.

Oh, man! Were we busted already? Did I just blow it?

"No, ma'am," I said, extra politely. "I have an identical twin sister who has you."

"Identical twins!" Mrs. Burkle said dramatically. "Ah, in literature twins are a recurring theme! From two sets of twins in Shakespeare's comedies, to the

Roman mythology of the twins Romulus and Remus, to the Bobbsey Twins . . ."

Mrs. Burkle wasn't even looking at me anymore. I steadied myself and slunk over to an empty desk in the back of the room. I hoped it was Payton's. It was in the back, where Payton usually sat. And no one told me to get up. Whew. I was safe. I was determined to fake my way through Payton's day. I mean, it was just Payton's life. How hard could it be?

Payton

(as Emma)

Thirteen

6TH PERIOD—EMMA'S STUDY HALL

I couldn't believe I'd embarrassed myself like that.

I walked quickly through the halls toward Emma's study hall. I looked down, avoiding eye contact with anyone who might look at me and think, *Hey! Isn't that Payton the Burrito Thrower?*

I was so embarrassed. No, I was HUMILIATED!

I was also dressed really, really badly. I was wearing Emma's navy sweats and peach sweatshirt. In public! Could this day get any worse?

Then I heard someone talking as she passed by.

"That's her twin in the sweats . . . burrito . . . so gross. You should have seen Sydney's face."

I ducked my head down and blinked back tears. I had really screwed up. Really really really screwed up.

I walked faster down the hall. And faster—and almost past Emma's study hall. The bell rang. I'd made it on time, just like I'd promised. I looked around. People were whispering. About me? I was so paranoid. I couldn't do this. There was no way I could survive Emma's study hall. Or Emma's choir. Or middle school.

I walked in, went straight over to the study hall monitor, and asked for a pass to the nurse's office. He didn't even look at me; just wrote out Emma's name when I told him. Whew.

"Name?" the nurse asked me.

"Pay—," I stopped myself. "I mean, Emma. Emma Mills."

"Problem?"

"I'm just—sick," I said.

"Your face is beet-red and flushed," the nurse announced. "And very sweaty. Likely a fever. Go lie down on the cot."

I took my sweaty red self over to the cot and lay down. I pulled the blanket over my face so nobody would recognize me. I was just going to hide out here and try not to think about burritos or mad friends or . . .

Mmmm . . .I had to admit these sweatpants were pretty soft and comfy. And this sweatshirt was fuzzy inside.

Ahhh. Snuggly.

I wiggled around until I got more comfortable.

And fell asleep.

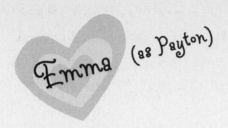
Emma (as Payton)

Fourteen

6TH PERIOD—PAYTON'S ENGLISH CLASS

"Man versus himself," I said.

Mrs. Burkle looked surprised.

"Correct, Payton," she said. "That *is* the conflict of this short story."

I was in Language Arts—again. It was the second time I'd heard this lesson today. Well, my real class had gone way more in depth into the symbolism and layers of meaning in this story. It *was* the advanced class. But it was the same story. Same conflict. Of course I knew the answer. And I thought Payton could use some bonus points in class for answering. I wouldn't overdo it, though.

During the rest of the class I memorized geography facts from a GeoBee study guide I'd grabbed off the book display on the way into class. I was sneak-reading under my desk. Huh. Who knew Vatican City was only .17 square miles?

I did, now.

"Miss Mills?" Mrs. Burkle said. "Please come up to my desk. Class, you have five free minutes of reading time."

Uh-oh. I dropped the book into my—I mean Payton's—tote bag. I looked around and saw everyone else reading from the textbook. Did Mrs. Burkle catch me sneaking the GeoBee? Payton wouldn't be caught dead with that book.

Did Mrs. Burkle suspect it was really me and not my sister? I slunk up to the teacher's desk.

"Miss Mills? I have a question for you," Mrs. Burkle asked, in her loud voice so everyone could hear. Oh, no. She's definitely onto us.

Okay. WWPS? What would Payton say?

"Um. Uh. Nope?" I answered, trying to sound Paytonish.

"As you know, Emma is in my fourth-period advanced honors class," Mrs. Burkle said.

She said Emma! She still thought I was Payton! I wasn't busted!

"Emma!" Mrs. Burkle went on. "I had a chance to review her files. What a fabulous student! Not only is her spelling letter perfect, but her writing is sublime!"

Really? Well!

"I didn't have the chance to tell Emma today," Mrs. Burkle continued. "But I'd like her to consider joining the *Gecko News*."

Write for the newspaper? Yes! Yes!

"I know Emma would love to do it!" I said. *Because Emma would! Because I'm Emma!*

"Your sister is a talented writer," Mrs. Burkle said.

"Yes," I said. "Emma is an inspiration to me. You may not have noticed this yet, but she'll probably be your star student."

Hee. And hee. This was great. I could compliment myself all I wanted. Maybe I should take this further. Maybe I should bring up how Jazmine James wasn't really all that and—

Clang! The bell for class ended.

"Class dismissed!" Mrs. Burkle said, turning away.

I headed off to Dumb People Math. Oh, all right, regular Math. In the hall I texted Payton.

how was study hall? r u ok?

Payton didn't answer. Oh, well. She couldn't have messed up my study hall. No worries.

I sat through Payton's math class, answering one question when the teacher called on me. I answered it wrong. On purpose. I was supposed to be Payton, right?

It was kind of fun, not having to think for a change.

Except that my outfit itched like crazy.

In art class we did watercolors. My picture turned out kind of mushy because I used too much water and not enough color. But it was okay! I didn't have to be perfect today!

"Hi, Payton," a girl with dark brown hair said to me. She laid her artwork out on the drying table next to mine.

"Hi . . ." I spotted her name on her painting. Quinn.

"Your picture is amazing!" I told her.

Quinn smiled. "Thanks. I love art."

The bell rang and everyone left the room.

how r u? remember: don't go to my math class!

Still no response. Payton was probably checking in at the nurse's office right about then. No problem. I'd just see her at the lockers. Meanwhile, I had one more class to pull off: PE.

PE was the major one. Sydney was in Payton's PE class. I'd have to face her.

I had Payton's PE clothes in her tote bag, so I went to the locker room to change. I couldn't wait to get out of those silly Summer Slave clothes! Then I saw Payton's PE clothes. They were Summer Slavewear too.

I sighed. I walked into the locker room and it went quiet.

About thirty girls had gone silent and were staring at me.

What? What?!

And then one girl spoke.

"Wow, you're actually here, Payton," she said. "I didn't think you'd show your face after, you know, what happened at lunch."

"Hello, Sydney," I replied, walking past her to an empty area of the locker room.

"Payton . . . Sydney . . . Ox . . . humiliating . . ."

I heard bits and pieces of girl talk. Whatever. I tuned it out.

I put on the Summer Slave T-shirt and shorts. Sequins? Who wears sequins to PE? This was going to be very uncomfortable.

I went back out to the gym.

"You are so brave," a girl whispered to me.

"Okay, sure," I said, and shrugged. Brave? Ha! Brave is facing down the top mathletes in the state when you're down by just one point. This was only PE!

"Girls! Laps!" Coach Hoen blew her whistle.

Ugh. I can't believe I had to go to gym twice in one day. One way Payton and I were alike: We were uncoordinated, so PE was not our specialty.

And this time I couldn't even talk my way out of it, because I had to prove to everyone that Payton was not hiding in shame.

"Laps, ew!" I said loudly enough for the girls (but not my teacher) to hear me. "This is so not my day!"

I walked out on the gym floor, holding my head high. I remember Payton saying she smiled a lot, so I slapped a smile on my face.

"Five times around the gym!" Coach Hoen yelled.

My smile faded. I sighed and went to the starting line. I stood right next to Sydney. I noticed her friends shift uncomfortably.

Coach Hoen blew the whistle and we started running. Sydney took off at the front of the pack. Unfortunately for me, she was apparently athletic, too. I summoned my strength and caught up with her. I was on a mission: Redeem my sister's honor!

"I so hate laps, don't you guys?" I said, cheerfully to her and some girl next to her. I maneuvered myself in between the two of them.

"I bet you do, since you can hardly walk without spilling things," the other girl said, in a snotty voice.

Sydney laughed.

"Just to inform you," I said to the other girl. "You need a tissue."

Sydney looked at the other girl and laughed again.

"Heh! You so have a huge booger," Sydney told her.

The girl turned red and ran off to the girls' room. Now it was just me and Sydney. I could feel my legs killing me, but I was not giving up. And was it my imagination, or was Sydney slowing down?

"So," Sydney finally spoke.

"So," I said cheerfully.

"You've got some nerve, Payton," Sydney said. "Hanging out with me like it's nothing. I mean, you haven't even apologized!"

Grr. *I* had to apologize? For what? Being insulted and called a fashion emergency? I had to stay calm. I had to do this for Payton.

"I don't like being yelled at," Sydney went on. "I definitely don't like people embarrassing our lunch table."

"I know," I improvised. "It's just . . . I'm kind of sensitive about my sister. She is my sister, you know."

"Well, it would be hard to have Emma for a twin," Sydney said.

Ergh. She was seriously getting on my nerves. Payton owed me big time for this. A small bunch of girls passed us. Whew. We were now in the middle of the pack. I couldn't keep up with the leaders anymore. My legs were feeling seriously wobbly. But I had to keep going. For Payton.

"Yeah," I said. "Just imagine if *you* had a sister who didn't like fashion or care about being cool!"

"I could see how that would put you over the edge," Sydney said, nodding. She was definitely breathing heavily. Not as athletic as I'd first thought.

I tried to think of what else I could say to wear Sydney down to forgive Payton. WWPD? What would Payton do . . . ?

"Sydney, I looove your shirt," I tried. "It's so . . . "

So *what*? I'd never really complimented anyone's shirt before. It was just some stupid gym shirt with some logo on it. Oh! I recognized the logo from an article I'd read online in my business journal—

" . . . cool. Isn't that from CocoBella's new fitness line?"

"Yeah—yeah, it is," Sydney said eagerly. "You know CocoBella's fitness line?"

"I heard they're coming out with sneakers in December," I recalled. "They're organic and great for the environment."

Wait. That didn't sound Paytonish.

"Plus!" I squealed. "They're soooo cute!"

Huh. I could never squeal before.

"Really? I didn't know that! It's not on their website yet," Sydney said. "How do you know that?"

I have to admit, I did feel a teeny bit proud of myself for my knowledge.

I shrugged. "I have my ways." *Financial Week* magazine, but I wasn't going to tell her that. "Exclusive insider information, you know. But let's keep that to ourselves."

"Speaking about keeping to ourselves . . ." Sydney looked around and lowered her voice. "Can you share any of that exclusive inside information with, say, one person?"

Hmm. Whatever could she be getting at?

"Weeeell . . ." I played hard to get. "I never have shared my scoop before. I always hoped I'd find someone to share my insider information with—like a special BFF."

BFF! That was such a Payton word. Heh! I was gooood. I jogged a little faster than Sydney, ignoring the ache in my legs.

"Wait! Payton!" Sydney called out. I slowed down and let her catch up to me.

"I never wanted our little misunderstanding at the lunch table to get in the way of our growing friendship," Sydney said. "I really feel like we got so close, so fast. You know, like we *were* BFFs."

How convenient.

"So! I'm ready to forgive you," Sydney announced.

Forgive me? Forgive me for being insulted and called a fashion emergency? I took a deep breath to stay calm. *Remember the goal, Emma. It's all for Payton.* I'd done well so far. It was like the final round of a debate competition. I had to finish this off for the win.

"Yay!" I said, in what I hoped was a perky voice. "We'll have so much fun being friends!"

"Then let's get together and talk fashion, 'kay?" Sydney said eagerly.

Sure thing. Whatever you say, Friend of Payton.

Tweeeeeet! Coach Hoen blew the whistle. "Less chatting, more running next time," she said right at Sydney and me.

"Yeah, right? And sweat? No, thank you," whispered Sydney, smiling at me.

"Sweat, ew," I said, nodding.

Gym class was over. My work here was done. I started to walk off the track. And I heard Sydney call after me: "Hey Payton! Let's hang later! For . . . you know!"

Fashion insider info. Yeah, I knew.

"Bye, Sydney!" I called out to her, making sure everyone heard me. "Text me!"

"Bye, Payton!" Sydney said.

After Sydney said bye, four or five other girls yelled bye to me too.

Well, that was a success! I couldn't wait to tell Payton.

Fifteen

FRIDAY, AFTER SCHOOL

"I was great as you," Emma said confidently as we went upstairs into our bedroom. "I should have won an Oscar."

We'd run right up to our room after we got off the bus. We yelled hi to my mom and raced to our room so she wouldn't see us dressed as each other.

Emma immediately turned on our computer and logged in. She always started homework the second we got home.

I flopped down on Emma's bed. Since I was still Emma. Plus, her bed was neat, while mine was covered with stuff.

"There's nothing to be embarrassed about or worried about at school anymore," Emma continued. "I totally took care of Sydney and everything for you."

Yeah, right. Like Emma just went and fixed my disaster? No offense to Emma, but she's not exactly known for her social skills.

"Well, whatever happened, thanks. I have to admit, it felt good to have no pressure on me for a little while," I told her. "It was so relaxing being you."

"RELAXING?!" Emma yelped. "It's not relaxing! I don't usually nap the school day away in the nurse's office, you know."

The nurse had woken me up at dismissal time. I'd slept through sixth, seventh, eighth, and ninth periods!

"True," I said, sitting up. "But you get to wear these comfy clothes and not care about how you look or what other people think of you!"

I pointed at the schlumpy clothes I needed to take off. In a few minutes. I'd wear them just a little longer. I mean, they *were* comfy.

"It's just so hard being me!" I flopped back on Emma's bed. "It's hard keeping up with Sydney and everyone!"

"Oh, please," Emma scoffed. "Hard is getting straight As and planning to get into the best college and

❀ 143 ❀

beating Jazmine James for valedictorian. It's so easy being you. Name one stress you have."

"I have to show my face at school after throwing a gross burrito on one of the most popular guys at school," I said.

"So, big deal—you go apologize to the guy," Emma said. She was typing on the computer while she talked.

I lay there and stared at Emma's posters on her wall. We had a white room, but we'd decorated our sides differently. Her comforter was denim blue and she had posters that said things like NEVER GIVE UP! She had study guides attached to her wall.

Honestly, it felt like I was in school.

My side of the room definitely didn't look like school. I had a hot pink comforter with pink, orange, and silver pillows on it. I also had a fuzzy round chair and a hot pink lava lamp, and the pictures on my walls were of singers, TV stars, and cute puppies. No study guides.

"Okay, here's the thing," I said. "So everyone loves Ashlynn's clothes—which they think are my clothes, right? I'm expected to look good. I have an image now. Well, it's getting cold out! I only have Summer Slave clothes! I can't afford 'in' clothes! And besides, I don't even know what's 'in' next! What am I supposed to wear? Everyone's going to know I'm a poser!"

Augh! I was doomed! I pulled the pillow over my head. I thought about ways I could convince my parents to let me switch schools.

"Okay, you can come out now," Emma said.

"I know you're going to tell me that I was shallow and superficial," I said. "But I was feeling like part of a group, you know? I liked it."

"I wasn't even going there," Emma said. "Here. I have an outfit for you."

I stuck my head out from under the pillow. Emma had laid out some clothes on my bed.

"Just wear your shirts layered like this." Emma pointed to two shirts layered in an unusual way.

"And these shoes you definitely have to wear," Emma said, pointing to a pair of gray sneakers.

They were a pair of sneakers that, honestly, I thought were kind of bluh. But if they were Ashlynn's, they must be in fashlynn. I mean in fashion. I hadn't even thought about wearing them. *But hey. Wait a minute. Since when is Emma giving me—or anybody—fashion advice?*

"Okay, I get why *you* like the sneakers," I said. Emma usually wore kind of boring colors. "But why did you layer the shirts like that?"

"That's the next trend," Emma said. "Just wear it and you'll be the first. Isn't that what you people care about?"

"How do you know that that's the next trend?" I asked.

"I just did a little Internet research," Emma said, turning the computer screen toward me.

I saw models and clothes on the screen. Huh? Emma was on a fashion website?

"This is depressing," I moaned. "You even make a better Payton than I do."

"Yes, I am doing a rather good job, aren't I?" Emma said. "I have to admit, it's actually kind of fun being you."

"How nice for you," I said. "Except that I'm not having fun being me anymore! I'm stressed! I'm supposed to be the laid-back, happy twin! You're the twin who's always a stress mess!"

"I'm not a stress mess!" Emma said. "Well, maybe I am. But I won't be for long. I actually got a ton of studying done today in your classes. I blew through the seventh-grade mathletics challenge study book *and* got some extra GeoBee study in during your classes. I've got the competitive edge now! It was like having a day of study hall."

"Hey! My classes aren't *that* easy," I told her.

Well, I guess they were for Emma. I was in the

"dumb" track. Well, that wasn't the official name, of course, but we all knew what it really was. I had a sneaking suspicion that if it weren't for me, Emma would have been skipped a grade. But me, the dumb one—I was holding her back.

I'd always wondered what it would be like to be as smart as Emma. So smart you could not pay attention and still have good grades. So smart you could be in a class and not sit there confused and then later feel stupid because you didn't understand what the heck the teacher was talking about.

It would be nice.

"Sometimes I wish I were you," I said. "You're so smart, and you win everything! I wish I could be like that for even one day."

"Well, sometimes I wish I were you," Emma said. "You're so laid-back, and you have lots of friends! I'd like to be that more too."

"What if we switched places?" We both said it out loud. At exactly the same time.

"TWINX!" we both yelled.

We said "TWINX" instead of "jinx" when we said something at the same time. Get it? Okay, dumb twin humor.

Next we got quiet.

Could we? Should we?

"No, that would be crazy," said Emma. "We can't switch again."

"No, we can't . . . ," I agreed.

Then I thought about showing my face again at school on Monday.

"Or maybe . . . we could?" I looked at Emma's face. She was looking back at me.

"Do you think we could get away with it?" Emma said. "Do you think people will really believe you're me? And I'm you?"

And then the door opened. And we both jumped.

"Hi, girls!" It was our mom. "How was your day at school?"

Uh . . .

"Interesting," I said.

"Eventful," Emma said.

"Well, you left your cell phones on the table downstairs," my mom said. "Here's yours, Payton."

I held out my hand. But Mom went past me and handed it to Emma.

"Emma, here's yours," my mom handed me Emma's cell phone.

"Thanks," I said.

"We'll be down in a little bit," Emma said.

Mom left and shut the door.

I looked at Emma, wearing my clothes, her hair brushed, and looking cute in my shiny lip gloss. She looked at me, wearing her clothes.

"She totally thought we were each other," Emma said, in amazement. "Even our own mother!"

"It's a sign!" I said. "A sign that we should switch."

"Maybe we should," Emma said. "But just for one day. I don't want you to ruin my grades."

"And I don't want you to ruin my social life," I shot back. *Oh, wait. I already did a good job of that myself.*

"I won't," Emma said. "Not only did I wow Sydney with my awesome Payton skills, I also said hello to four people in my classes. I was extremely extroverted."

"You didn't really say 'hello,' did you?" I asked. "You mean 'hi' or 'hey,' right?"

"Well, no," Emma said. "I said 'hello.' But don't worry, I also mixed it up and said 'good afternoon.'"

Okay, that was just weird. She couldn't do that anymore.

"Just stick with 'hi,'" I said.

Emma sighed and got up and bounced across the

room. She turned toward my Jonas Brothers poster.

"Hi!" she said, in a fake voice. "I'm Payton! I only speak Kewl!"

"Lame imitation," I said. "Fake, phony, and poserish. Smile because you actually like people!"

"Fine, I'll like people," Emma said. "Hi!" She flashed a huge smile at me. "I'm sooo happy to see you!"

"Not bad," I said.

"Well, *you* I'm happy to see," Emma said. "Your so-called friends, not so much."

"Former friends," I said. *Former friends who will probably never speak to me again.*

"Did you talk to Quinn, Cashmere, or Priya today?"

"I don't know." Emma shrugged. "Do I really have to tell them apart? Can't I just call them Sydney Wannabes One, Two, and Three?"

"No!" I said. "You can't. Remember, you have to be nice. I'm a nice person. And you're me."

"FINE. I'll be nice," Emma said. "What else?"

"You also have to stay looking cute. Go to the locker or girls' room after every class. Brush your hair; check your teeth for gross things stuck in them."

"After every class?" Emma said. "You waste a lot of valuable study time. So what else do I need to know? I

already know your schedule, teacher names, and classrooms."

Emma had memorized my schedule the first day and
quizzed me till I knew it, too. Hmm.

"Don't flirt with guys named Cameron, Mac, Justin,
Noah, or Griffin," I said thoughtfully. "They're Sydney's."

"Flirt?" Emma asked. "I'm not flirting with anybody! Don't go all crazy now."

"Okay, let's practice," I said. "Show me your best
Payton."

Emma left the room. And bounced back in.

"Wait. Do I really bounce like that when I walk?" I
asked her.

"Yes," she said. "You also push your hair behind your
ears like this. And chew on your lip."

Emma pushed her hair behind her ears and chewed
on her lip.

"Hi!" she said, waving at me. "Um, I'm Payton.
Oooh, I just love those shoes!"

And then she flashed a smile.

"Whoa," I told her. "That was so me it's scary."

Emma beamed, all proud.

"Thanks!" she said. "Anything else? Study material?"

"Well, okay," I said. I looked around my side of the

room. "Here are some teen magazines. A list of the newest most popular downloads on iTunes. And you can go through the pictures on my phone and I'll tell you who's who."

"That's a start," Emma said. "By Monday, I *will* be Payton!"

"And now, I need to become Emma," I said. I took a deep breath and stood in front of her in the middle of my room.

"What do I need to know?" I asked. "Who should I talk to? Who are the important people in your life?"

"These people," Emma said. She dragged her ginormous backpack over to me. She reached in and pulled out a sheet of paper.

Schedule   Emma Mills   Grade 7

"My teachers," Emma said. "Memorize all their names. And my class schedule. And here's a map of my classes and a layout of where I sit in each class. I made that for myself since I didn't have front row center anymore. See? The star symbol is me."

"Okay," I said. "What else?"

"That's it," Emma said.

"That's it?" I protested. "That can't be all!"

"Oh, you're right!" she said. "There's one more important thing."

She went over to our computer and typed something up. She printed it off our printer.

"Ten copies," she said. "Just hand one of these to each of my teachers. And one to Jazmine James, so she doesn't think I'm being quiet because I don't know the answers."

I looked at the paper.

Dear Teacher,

I so long to participate in your class; however, I have a severe case of otolaryngitimis. My physician assures me it is not contagious and my voice should be back by school day tomorrow.

Sincerely,

Emma

P.S. I will do extra credit to compensate for my lack of verbal participation today.

"What's otolary-huh? Do I really have it?" I asked.

"Duh, Payton, I made it up," Emma said. "It means you have a sore throat and can't talk. So basically, just don't say a word."

"I don't get to talk?"

"It's the only way to make sure I don't look dumb. No offense," Emma added quickly. "Just make sure you look at the teacher, and look like you're paying attention. And use this."

Emma gave me her mini-recorder.

"Record every lesson," Emma said.

"Got it," I said. "And what else? Any people to know about? Like . . . friends?"

"Pshaw. Don't let people distract you from your mission," Emma said dismissively. "Especially people like Jazmine, Hector, and Tess. Focus on the teacher and record the lesson."

"Um, okay," I said. I didn't know who Hector or Tess were, but I guess it didn't matter since I was supposed to ignore them. "I guess I'm ready to be you right now. Okay! Here I am! Emma Mills!"

I did my best impression of Emma. I slouched my shoulders and hunched over like I had a big backpack on me. I frowned and wrinkled my forehead.

"What do you think?" I asked Emma. "Am I you or what?"

"I do *not* look like that," Emma protested. "I don't look like that at all!"

Just then our door opened.

"Dinner's ready," my mom said. "And Emma, here's that permission slip you need for your science fair."

And she handed it to me.

The door closed behind her as she left.

"HA!" I said. "She thought I was you. You *do* look like that."

"Hmph," Emma said. "Whatever. Wait, my hair feels crooked. Can you help me make it look right?"

"I think you're on your way to making an excellent me," I said. I went over to help her fix the part in her hair.

And it hit me when I saw our reflections.

I looked at Emma in my clothes, adjusting her hair in my mirror. I saw myself in Emma's sweats with my hair in a ponytail.

We were more than just trading places. We were trading faces.

Emma
(as Payton)

Sixteen

MONDAY, HOMEROOM

Lip gloss! Oh, no!

Did I forget Payton's lip gloss? I opened her tote, felt around, and—whew! I found it! Without it I couldn't be Payton.

As I walked into Homeroom 220, I realized:

- ☑ Payton's tote bag was really light and easy to carry around.
- ☑ I wouldn't have to think so hard for a change today.
- ☑ Jazmine James wasn't in any of Payton's classes.

Being Payton = one day of:

Carefree! Brainfree!
And Jazminefree!
Hee!
"Hi, Payton!" a girl said to me.
"Hi!" I looked at her and flashed her a big friendly smile. Just the way Payton had coached me.
"Payton, hey!" A boy nodded at me.
"Hey!" I nodded back. Maybe Emma was tongue-tied around boys, but Payton wasn't. Okay, so maybe I only said one word, but still.
I walked to the back of the room and saw her: Payton's frenemy, Sydney. I breezily walked past her and nodded confidently. I sat in the desk behind her. Homeroom was fifteen minutes long, just long enough to review my Spanish tenses. I closed my eyes to run through a few.
"Ohmigosh, Payton!"
Ugh. It was Sydney. I opened my eyes to see her turned around, looking at me.
"You are such a liar!" she said.
Huh?

"You said CocoBella wasn't coming out with their sneaker line till December," Sydney said. "You didn't tell me you already snagged a pair!"

I was wearing the ones I'd shown Payton Friday night.

"Um . . ." I held up my foot to show off Ashlynn's/Payton's shoe. "I . . . It's . . ."

"Silence!" the homeroom teacher yelled, saving me from having to come up with an answer.

Sydney turned back around.

I could now continue my Spanish tenses.

"Ow!" A square of paper hit me in the forehead and landed on my desk. What now? I opened it.

I totally love those shoes, the note said.

Um, okay. That was worth a note and a potential bruise to my forehead? I sent her one back.

Thanks.
☺

Payton always added smiley faces to her notes. I'd had one this morning from her in my/her tote bag:

Don't be hatin'
Today you're Payton!

xo "Emma" ☺

Lame poem, but a nice thought. *Oh, great.* Another note landed on my desk.

Can u hook me up with a pair?

Um . . . no.
I scribbled a little note on Payton's pink pad and tossed it over Sydney's shoulder.

I'll see what I can do. P. ☺

Sydney turned around and smiled.
I'll see what I can do? I can do nothing. But it kept Sydney happy for now, so hey. I'd accomplished my main goal as Payton, and it was only, what, 7:12 in the morning? Sydney wouldn't mess with my sister as long as she believed those silly sneakers were coming. And hopefully Payton would weasel her way back into the Kewl Clique or whatever it was they called themselves, and Sydney would forget all about the sneakers.
"Mills, Payton? Mills, Payton?"
A boy next to me kicked my chair.

"Oh! Present! I mean, here!" I said loudly. Oops. I know Payton wasn't known for paying attention but I'm sure she never screwed up answering for attendance.

I focused on my Spanish homework.

Another note flew on to my desk.

If they have them in gray get those! Size 7.

Oh, righty, I'll just race right out and—
Clang! Clang! Clang!

The bell rang. Rats. I'd only conjugated half my verbs, thanks to Sydney's incessant note throwing. No wonder Payton never got much done in school, if people were always interrupting her with notes and other trivialities.

"Bye, Payton!" Sydney called out.

"Bye, Payton!" a chorus of Sydneyites followed.

"Bye!" I smiled, waved in a friendly way, and walked out of homeroom.

Now I had a morning full of easy classes. What a day. Suck up to Sydney? Accomplished. Now it was time to study. Starting, appropriately with study hall.

Next I went to second-period Science. It was easy. I got to study the rest of my Spanish tenses. Yes! I mean, *sí*!

Third-period French? *Facile*. Which means easy.

*Looks like I'll be learning two languages this year. Wait,
three—I'm getting pretty good at speaking Payton.* I said hi
to three people and used "um" and "yeesh" a lot.

Fourth-period Social Studies. Easy peasy.

But now came the true test: lunch. Just last week I'd
spent lunch in the library, sneaking little bites of food
from behind a book.

"Payton! Over here!" Sydney beckoned me to her
table.

Now . . . I was going to eat with some of the most
popular people in school.

I said "some," not "all." Because yesterday I'd noticed
another group of oh-so-pretty girls, all of them wearing
Geckos Cheerleading jackets. And there they were, on
the other side of the cafeteria, sitting *with* boys. Who
were also in Gecko jackets.

And here I was, in Payton's own little corner of
cool.

I was a little nervous, but I was ready. Over
the weekend I had approached the study of cool as if I
were cramming for a competition. I'd Googled, blog-
hopped, studied, and memorized. I'd created one file
called Popularology and one called Trends.

Then I'd moved on to Payton's magazines. Fashions!

Tweens! Crushes! Most embarrassing moments!

Okay, I'm an overachiever. But we already knew that. What I hadn't known was that there was a whole world of information available to help me become a typical tween.

Like Payton.

"Hi, Payton," waved one of the girls at Sydney's table. I smiled and sat down amongst Queen Sydney and her Court.

They were all talking nonstop, so I just ate my lunch without saying pretty much anything. Occasionally I nodded and went "Uh-huh! Yeah! Totally!" Just agree with the group—that was the way to fit in.

And then Sydney mentioned a shirt she'd bought at a store I'd never been to but I had seen advertised so much in Payton's magazines that I felt like I'd been there a million times.

"It's icy gray with long sleeves and a little lace around the neck," Sydney said. "I'm trying to think of what to wear with it to the concert this weekend."

"How about a rose-pink bead choker, wide-leg jeans, and silver ballet flats?" I suggested. "And a signature piece—like a chocolate-brown bag?"

The whole table turned to stare at me.

"Or," I continued, "you could go natural with a rope belt, hemp headband, and natural-colored shirt."

"Payton, wow," said the bouncy, brown-haired girl I'd met in Payton's art class on Friday. Quinn. "You so have to come shopping with us!"

I thought back to the cheat sheet Payton had given me. Quinn was the nicest one. I smiled at her.

"She could be like our personal shopper," Cashmere said. Not the nicest FOS (Friend of Sydney), according to the cheat sheet. "Right, Syd? Like, she could work for us?"

Nice attempt to put me down. I did not smile at her.

Sydney looked at me.

"We're going to the mall after school," Sydney said. "You should come, Payton."

"Um, sure," I said, thinking. Payton and I would have to switch back right at dismissal time, but I could probably make it. I meant, she could.

I sat back, satisfied. I'd gotten Payton invited to the mall. She'd be happy when I told her. I was more than a little impressed with myself, tossing out the fashion advice like that. All that research had paid off. As soon as Sydney had said icy gray with long sleeves, I'd remembered seeing that shirt in *Teen Twist* (page 31) with the beads and jeans and flats and the headline about shaking it up with the handbag. And I'd read online how accessorizing with natural materials and neutral colors was about to be a trend.

My near-photographic memory was coming in handy, even if it was for shallow, superficial things.

Just then, four boys came over to our table.

"Hey," they said.

Sydney and the girls got all flirty-flirty. I just sat there. I wondered what Payton would do. I had no clue, so I hoped the boys would go back to boy land.

Instead, I nearly got shoved off my chair by a guy.

"Shove over," the boy said. "Make room for the stud."

I was supposed to share a seat with someone who called himself the stud?

"Oh, please, Mac," Sydney said.

"Be careful of her," Cashmere said. "She might throw a burrito at you like she did at Ox."

Everyone laughed.

"I could take it," said the boy sitting diagonally across from me. Oh! He was—

"Burrito boy!" The words tumbled out of my mouth before I could stop them.

"I was on Friday," he said. "Usually I'm Ox."

"I'm so, so sorry," I said. "It was an accident, and I'd be happy to clean your shirt."

"Nah," Ox said. "My mom took care of it. No biggie."

Ox stood up and stretched. Hmm. He wasn't too tall. Or too short. He was just nice, but in a muscly way. I would have thought someone named Ox would be huge and wide. And with a name like Ox, of course he was a dumb jock.

But, um. He was cute.

"Ox," Cashmere said, "did you know that when you write your name, it's like a hug and a kiss? *O* and *X*, get it?"

"Ooooh, Ox." The boys next to me started making kissing sounds. "You're so sweet."

Sydney rolled her eyes and stood up.

"Puh-lease, he's a big strong guy," Sydney said.

"Yea! Oxes are big and strong," Cashmere added.

"Oxen," Ox and I said at the same time.

"What?"

"The plural of 'ox' is oxen," I explained. "Not 'oxes.'"

"Whatever," Cashmere said, looking annoyed.

"No, she's right," Ox said. "Oxen."

Holy moley. He was looking right at me. Our eyes

held for a few seconds. He had big brown eyes with long lashes. I looked away.

I blushed.

"Payton, I have the best idea! In gym we can trade sneakers," Sydney said. "Don't you guys think those CocoBella sneakers are so me?"

"*So* you," I agreed. And so not me. They were starting to pinch my feet. Another difference between me and Payton: two shoe sizes.

The boys left, apparently not fascinated by the sneaker-swapping discussion. Soon after, lunch ended and we took off. We emptied our garbage and passed by the Gecko jacket area.

"Hi, guys!" Sydney said to their table. A couple of the cheerleaders looked up.

"Oh, hi, Cindy," said one of them.

Sydney kept her grin on, and we walked out of the cafeteria.

"You spent so much time practicing with them this summer, you'd think they'd remember your name, Sydney," Cashmere said.

"Whatevs," Sydney said. "No biggie. No big deal. Nope, not a big deal at all."

I glanced at her. She was gritting her teeth in a frozen smile. Obviously, it was bothering her. Interesting.

"Seriously," Cashmere said, "just because you didn't make the squad doesn't mean they have to act like that . . ."

"I said shut it, Cashmere," Sydney said, her smile fading. But she flashed it back on, full wattage, when a nice-looking boy walked by.

"Hi, Tyson," she said.

"Hey, Sydney," the boy said, nodding back.

"He's in eighth grade," Sydney informed me. And we all split up to go to sixth period. I had plenty of time to go to the lockers before English class.

Payton's locker opened. I peered into the monstrosity. The lights blinked; the fluffy decorations made my eyes blurry. I pushed back the books and notebooks that were falling out and took a look in the mirror, as I'd promised Payton I would.

Teeth? Check. Hair? Good. It was so weird to look in the mirror at myself and see my sister. I saw the *P* from her bracelet reflecting in the mirror.

I was about to shut the locker, when I saw a boy's face in the mirror.

Ox!

I turned around, and there he was.

Ox!

Oh! Um! Oh!

My mind went blank. What do I do? What do I say? It's Ox! All I could think about was a bizarre flashback to the *Animal Encyclopedia for Kids* I'd read when I was little. I pictured an ox in the *O* section.

"So! Did you know that oxen are really just huge, trained cattle?" I said.

Okay, I can't believe I just said that. Even I knew that was dorky. And definitely something Payton would never ever have said.

He just looked at me.

"Uh-huh," he said.

Maybe he was smarter than his name suggested. Maybe he wasn't. But I didn't care! With that wavy brown hair and great smile, who needed brains?!

Did I just think that?!

"Actually, they're also intelligent and hardworking," Ox said. "But in poor countries they're treated pretty badly."

"They are?" I asked. "How do you know that?"

"I wrote a report on them in third grade," he said. "It got me pretty mad to read about how they were treated. I ended up making everyone donate their allowances to this ox foundation. I know, it sounds pretty goofy."

"Actually, it sounds nice," I said.

❀ 168 ❀

"Well, anyway, that's how I got my nickname," Ox said.

Wow. I'd assumed it was because he played the sport where guys smashed into each other like big, dumb animals.

"Yo, Ox!" some guy yelled. "Coach wants to see us. Something about practice."

"Dude," Ox said to him. And then he turned to me. "Later."

That was . . . interesting. I shut Payton's locker, but not before getting swopped in the face by her hanging beads.

I felt a little woozy, but whether it was from the beads or from the exchange with Ox, I wasn't sure.

Um. *Get a grip, Emma. Get a grip.*

I took a deep breath and headed to Payton's English class.

Payton
(as Emma)

Seventeen

MONDAY, NINTH PERIOD

Calculator! Did I forget my calculator?

I opened Emma's backpack. If I was going to sit through Emma's math class, I'd better have a calculator on standby. Ouch! I just got stabbed by a sharp something. What the heck . . . ?

I pulled out a pencil. It was the sharpest pencil ever. That shouldn't have surprised me. Sometimes I'd be sleeping and I'd hear this *wzzzzt, wzzzzt* noise. It was Emma, up at like midnight, sharpening her pencils.

But I wasn't used to getting stabbed by them. I carefully reached in and found the calculator. Okay, I was ready for last period.

My day had gone pretty well. I had handed out the notes explaining I had otolaryngitisomething. In each class I sat in my seat, turned on the tape recorder, and shut up. I had no clue what was going on in her classes. I wished we had written that I also had a sleeping sickness. I had a seriously hard time trying to stay awake, and then I could have put my head down on my desk.

Emma had instructed me to stay away from the lunchroom, which would be my greatest chance of being discovered. She'd told me how to get an honors pass for the library instead. It meant choking down a granola bar behind the librarian's back, but it was worth it not to have to try to be Emma at lunch.

Choir was easy too, with my "illness." Emma told me she always mouthed the words anyway. Have I mentioned that Emma can't sing? It's painful.

So, eight periods down and one to go. Math.

Math would definitely be my hardest class of the day. I mean, could you stay awake with a bunch of math brainiacs going "One gajillion squared divided by thirty-seven equals blah blah blah?"

I wasn't sure I'd be able to either.

I walked into math class. I checked my notes for the

teacher's name: Mr. Cuyler. How did you pronounce that? Oh, well, it didn't matter; I wouldn't be speaking.

"Hi!" I said to a girl I recognized from Choir. I said it kind of hoarsely, the way I imagined someone with otolaryngitis would talk. I'd been talking like this all day. At first it was kind of fun, like I was an actress playing the role of someone with a terrible illness that had stolen her voice. But now, by the end of the day, it was just making my throat sore.

The girl gave me a weird look. Huh. I thought she was that girl who'd stood next to me in Emma's choir class, but maybe I'd mixed her up with someone else. Maybe she had an identical twin too.

I found Emma's seat and sat down. I recognized the guy behind me from Emma's homeroom that morning.

"Hey," I turned around and said to the guy.

He didn't hear me.

"HEY," I said louder.

"Yes?" he looked up, expectantly.

"Just saying hi," I said.

"You are?" he asked. "Why?"

"Um, to be friendly?" I said.

"Okay," he shrugged. "That's a first."

❀ 172 ❀

"I've never said hi to you before?" I asked him. Uh-oh. Maybe Emma didn't like him. Maybe he was a mean person.

"No offense, but you haven't talked to me since the first homeroom," he said. "In fact I've never seen you say hi to anyone."

Really? Emma never said hi to anyone? Maybe that's why people were giving me weird looks when I said hi to them! That explained a lot! Except that that didn't seem very friendly of Emma.

Aha! This was my chance! I could improve Emma's reputation! I could spend the rest of the day—okay, all one hour of it—saying hi to people! Then people would know Emma really was a nice person!

"I've had this case of otolaryngitis," I explained to him. "So it's hard for me to say hi sometimes."

I coughed dramatically to prove the point.

"You talk a lot when teachers call on you," he said, looking confused.

Oh. That.

"Uh. It comes and goes," I said. "And um, I have to save my voice for class and—"

Oh, just forget it. I give up.

"Whatever! Boring topic!" I smiled brightly, trying

to change the subject. "What do you think of the math teacher?"

"I think you'd better turn around," he whispered. "Because he's here."

Oops. I turned around as Mr. Cuyler came in. Everyone quieted down and started to focus their math-genius minds on what the teacher was saying.

Except me. I opened up my books and turned on Emma's mini-recorder. *La la la.* Forty-five minutes to kill. I leaned back in my seat. I had to admit, if I didn't look down at what I was wearing and see the hideousness, Emma's sweats were an extremely comfortable way to lounge through the school day.

La la la. Doo dee doo.

Ouch! The guy behind me kicked me. Okay, maybe that's why Emma never said hi to him, because he kicked her. I turned around to shoot him a dirty look.

"You're being called on," he whispered at me.

Oh! I tuned back in to the teacher.

"MILLS! Emma Mills, are you with us today?" the teacher was saying.

People were giggling.

"Yes!" I said. "Yes, I am!"

Okay, no teachers were supposed to call on me! I had the excuse note and—

Oh, dang it. The teacher had come in late, and I'd totally forgotten to give him the otolaryngitis note.

"Then kindly share the answer to question twelve," he said.

I coughed dramatically.

"Sorry!" I rasped. "I can't speak today. I have a throat illness."

"Then why don't you come up to the chalkboard and demonstrate in writing," the teacher said. "Question 12."

Uh. Oh.

I was supposed to lay low! Lay low! This was not good. I couldn't ruin Emma's reputation. She would not be happy.

"Ms. Mills!" the teacher said. "To the front."

I picked up the textbook, pushed my chair back, and made my way to the front of the class. The teacher handed me a piece of chalk. This couldn't be good.

I stood there doing nothing except looking around wildly for rescue. But all I saw was Jazmine James, sitting in the front row with a big smirk on her face. The guy and girl sitting next to her were cracking up at me. I stalled for time by copying the problem very slowly on the board.

And then I heard Jazmine James say something under her breath: "Isn't this supposed to be the *smart* class?"

Okay, that was just plain mean. I was used to not knowing the answer, but not to people being so mean about it.

I looked at Jazmine, sitting there all smug. Errgh.

"You may not have heard what Jazmine said, so I'll repeat it," I said to the class, my voice wavering a little. "She said, 'Isn't this supposed to be the smart class?'"

I ignored Jazmine's glare and kept going.

"Yes, Jazmine James," I said, looking right at her. "We *are* in the smart class, and it's way awkward that I'm standing up here without an answer. But come on, guys, haven't you ever had that moment when you're stuck feeling stupid because you don't know an answer?"

Everyone looked at me blankly. Okay, maybe since they were geniuses they always knew the answer. The teacher even looked confused.

"Okay, then." I kept trying. "Haven't you ever felt stupid when you . . . um . . . walked into a party or . . . or . . . went to a new after-school competition club and didn't know what to do? And felt like everyone was staring at you and you were hoping nobody was laughing at you?"

I noticed the girl sitting next to Jazmine James

nodding. And then a couple more heads were nodding. I glanced at the teacher, who didn't seem to be planning to stop me, so I kept going.

"And haven't you ever wished someone would just help you out of that awkward situation?" I said louder.

More nodding heads. Oh, yeah! I was on a roll, baby!

"But instead of help, what Jazmine James offered was a put-down! A put-down, so everyone would stare and laugh! It's all of our worst nightmares come true, isn't it? Now, Jazmine, was there any need to be hurtful to a fellow classmate in her time of need?"

"No!" someone called out.

"So let me be the first to say, HELP! I don't know this answer—but it's okay! *I* am going to ask for help! Jazmine James, will you please help me with this math problem? Please do not insult me! Please help me, your classmate, in my time of need!"

I held out my chalk to Jazmine. She looked slightly stunned. She looked around the class and obviously sensed defeat. She stood up without looking at me and took the chalk. Then she went up to the chalkboard and started writing out the answer.

And I held my head up high and walked to the back row. But not before some geeky guy held out his hand for me to high-five. I high-fived him and took my seat again.

Whew! At least I didn't

a) get Emma in trouble

and more importantly

b) have to do that impossible math problem on the board.

Hopefully, Emma would never hear about this.

"Yes, Ms. James," the math teacher was saying, as he looked at Jazmine's answer on the chalkboard. "Your answer is correct. Class, homework will be pages fourteen and fifteen . . ."

And just then the bell rang. Whew and whew!

Class was over. Everyone started heading out the door. I needed to get out of this place quickly. I tried to blend in with the crowd, but—

"Ms. Mills?"

Drat. The teacher. I slunk over to the desk.

"Um," I said. "Hi?"

"That was an interestingly compelling little speech

you gave here," he said. "I must confess that I, too, have had those awkward moments—for example, when entering the teachers' lounge . . . but I digress. Next time I call on you, I'd like the answer to the math question."

"Yes, sir!" I said firmly. "Absolutely!"

I bolted out of the classroom and finally made my getaway . . .

SMACK!

. . . running right into someone. The boy who sat behind me was standing there. Well, half standing, since I'd practically knocked him over.

"Oof!" he said.

"Sorry!" I said. "I didn't see you!"

"I hope not," he said, rubbing his arm. "Or I'd be wondering why you intentionally tried to run me over when I was just waiting for you."

"You were waiting for me?" I asked him.

"I wanted to say that that was an interesting speech you gave up at the chalkboard," he said.

"Thanks, um . . ."

"Nick," he said. We started walking down the hall toward my locker.

"Well, obviously I choked up there," I said.

"I've never seen you choke before," he told me. "It's

nice to know that you actually are human."

"What?" I asked.

"I've seen you at a couple competitions, and it was like you had nerves of steel," he said. "Seeing you choke up there today just made you, I don't know, more approachable."

"Really?" I said. "So you've seen Emma—I mean me—before?"

"Yup," he said. We walked down the hall together. "You know, I've also seen you in a debate from the audience. My younger sister Margaret does a lot of competitions. She's only ten; she skipped two grades. My parents make me go for 'family spirit.' Margaret came in second to you at the spelling bee. So I'm not surprised you got yourself out of that answer today. That was pretty smart."

Really? Me? Today? Smart?

"Remember in that debate competition?" he said. "You said that the combination of solar panels and environmentally friendly landscaping is intelligent design . . ."

Wow, speaking of intelligent. As he babbled on about solar something, I had a brilliant idea.

Nick was smart and not horribly bad-looking with

his light brown buzz cut. Being brutally honest, he looked totally geek.

Which was awesome!

This could be a perfect love match for Emma! While Emma would turn purple if she had to talk to him, I could pave the way for her! I imagined them at the prom together, maybe being adorkable co-valedictorians, and—

"Emma?" Nick said. "Are you listening?"

"Oh! I was just imagining the possibilities!" I said. "Of . . . solar energy."

"Well, I was just saying it's cool you're doing this, too," Nick said, holding the door open for me as I walked through it into the classroom. "Let's grab a seat."

"Okay!" I said, as he took a seat near the front of the room and I sat down next to him and got ready to . . .

Got ready to . . .

Uh.

Uh.

Where was I? Why was I in this room?

Wait! I was supposed to be at my locker and getting on the bus!

AND MEETING EMMA!!! AND SWITCH-ING CLOTHES AND GOING BACK TO BEING PAYTON!!!!

!!!!

I looked around wildly. I grabbed my tote bag—no, Emma's backpack—to get up and—

"People! Please sit down!" Mrs. Burkle walked in the door.

I sat down. *Okay. Okay. What should I do?* I was supposed to be meeting Emma right now.

"Welcome, all my fine honors students, my best and brightest, to our new and improved media center, and to the first year of VOGS!" Burkle announced.

What the heck was VOGS? I think Mrs. Burkle had mentioned it in Emma's English class, but I'd forgotten what she said.

"VOGS stands for Videocast of Gecko Students," Burkle said. "A 'vodcast,' if you will. We will be preparing a video news show that will run the final fifteen minutes of every Friday. And the exciting part is that it will be shown *live*!"

Oh, now I remembered Mrs. Burkle asking me—well, Emma—to come to this meeting. So I guess Emma was supposed to be here. So that meant I was supposed to be here.

Plus, I'd already missed the bus. So I was stuck. I slouched down in my seat. Since I was here, I would just make myself comfortable. I slid Emma's phone out of the bag and sent her a text:

Burkle wanted u to come 2 a club thing so I got stuck. i m still u. u still be me. will take late bus home.

Fortunately my mom was at some meeting, so we were supposed to let ourselves in. Emma could just go home and nobody would know any better.

Mom. I'm staying after school for a club thing. Sincerely, Emma.

There. I hope that sounded Emma-ish.

I tuned back in.

"First off, if you are not a member of the honors program, please excuse yourselves," Burkle said.

A few people got up, looking disappointed. But not me! Because I was in the honors program! Well, at least today I was. Today, I was smart, honors, talented, and gifted Payton-Emma! Mills.

"And so are there any volunteers for our very first VOGS?" Mrs. Burkle was saying.

Oh! Whoops. I'd been spacing out. Volunteers for what? Well, Emma was always volunteering for everything. And look! There was that Jazmine girl with her hand up.

Emma would *not* want to lose out on anything to her.

I raised my hand high.

"Let's have Jazmine, DeShaun, Ahmad, and Emma as our first volunteers," Mrs. Burkle said.

Perfect! This was working out after all. Emma was going to be so happy with me. I looked around at all the high-tech computers, TV monitors, cameras, and lights. Emma was always talking about extracurriculars to help her get into the best college. Well, this place sure looked professional.

This was going to be like her dream come true.

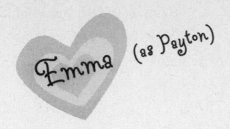
Emma (as Payton)

Eighteen

MONDAY, AFTER SCHOOL

I was in a nightmare.

Seriously, it was like a nightmare. Six Sydneys.

Okay, only one was really Sydney. The rest were reflections in mirrors.

"How do I look in this?" Sydney posed. She was up on a platform in the dressing room in the clothes store.

We were in some store in the mall that seemed to think the more mirrors the better. And of course Sydney seemed to agree.

"It's great!" said Quinn, who was standing on one side of me.

❀ 185 ❀

"Sydney looks great in everything," Cashmere said, from my other side.

Everyone looked at me, waiting for my compliment.

"Um," I said.

Six Sydneys turned to look at me.

"What?" Sydney said, with a little frown.

What? I was pretending to be Payton, which meant smiling and nodding and making people feel good. But I just couldn't do it this time.

"Your sweater just isn't . . . right," I told her. "It would work better if . . . wait. Don't move."

I ran out of the changing room, weaved through some racks, and grabbed a different, shorter sweater. On the way back I spotted a thin sweater and took it off the display. I'd seen this in one of the magazines, though never on anyone I knew.

"Try these," I said to Sydney, who was still standing up on the platform. Looking annoyed.

She took the clothes into the cubicle with a loud sigh. Sydney came out with the thin sweater on. "BO-ring," she announced.

"Wait," I said. "Now put the other sweater over it. And tie it like this . . ."

❀ 186 ❀

I tied the sweater belt a certain way, and—

"Wow," said Quinn. "Okay, that looks sweet."

Cashmere looked at Sydney, then at me. "For the accessories, we'll keep it simple," I said. "This silver link chain will do it." I slipped it over Sydney's head and stepped back to admire my work.

"I don't know," she said, looking at me. "I've never seen an outfit like *that* before."

Sydney twisted and turned and checked herself out from all angles.

"Yeah, Payton," she said. "Are you sure about this?"

I played with the *P* cuff around my wrist. WWPS?

Suddenly, a salesperson burst into the changing room.

"Oh, sorry, I thought this room was empty . . . ,"she said. Then she stopped.

"That is so fashion forward!" she exclaimed, looking at Sydney. "At our training conference one of the models was wearing something just like that. She looked so hot, just like you."

"Really?" Sydney said, obviously happy about being told she looked hot.

"In fact," the salesperson said, "our store is going to be pushing that look for next season!"

"Sydney, you'll be setting the style," Cashmere simpered. "As usual."

She conveniently ignored my part in all this.

The salesperson left, and Sydney hopped down from the platform.

"Payton, this is awesome," she said, linking her arm in mine. "Now you can go pick out an outfit for Quinn and Cash. And maybe two or three for you, too, of course."

Of course. Because, as Sydney and Cashmere had pointed out at least three times on the ride over to the mall, Payton was in desperate need of new clothes.

So why wasn't the *real* Payton here in the mall? Because the minute gym had let out, at dismissal time, Sydney had practically dragged me out of the side entrance of the school. Where Quinn and Cashmere were waiting so we could all jump in Sydney's mother's car and have her whisk us away for shopping.

It had all happened so fast. One minute I was in the gym; the next I was in the third-row seat of Sydney's SUV, texting Payton.

Change of plans! Explain later. C U at home. Stay me!!!

Then calling my mom.

"Hi, Mom, um, this is, um, Payton," I said. Everyone in the car could hear me.

"Oh, good," my mother had said. "I just heard from your sister."

My sister, Payton? Or "my" sister, "Emma?" It was seriously confusing.

"Uh . . . what did she say?" I'd asked.

"Emma's staying after school for an extracurricular, so she'll take the late bus home," Mom had said.

"Oh! I'll, uh, be a little late too," I told her. "I'm on my way to the mall. Sydney's mom is driving."

I had given my mom Sydney's mother's cell phone number and hung up. Payton was going to *what* after-school activity? Was she still pretending to be me? I hoped so, since otherwise there would be two Paytons at the same time in different places.

But if she *was* still being me, and I was still pretending to be her, how did this happen? We were supposed to switch back after last period!

But nobody could fight the force of Sydney on a mission. Thus here I was, in some store, picking out an outfit for, of all people, Cashmere.

"Try this." I handed her a shirt/pants/sweater

combo. Cashmere disappeared inside the dressing-room cubicle and then came out to stand on the platform in front of Sydney and Quinn. They looked her up and down.

I held my breath as I waited for their verdicts. My heart was pounding; my hands felt clammy. I wanted to chew on my hair, but that was not *kewl*. The last time I'd felt like this was . . .

The state spelling bee. Right before the judges announced if my word was correct or dinged the loser bell if it was wrong. I'd never been dinged that day.

But today? Would I get dinged?

Sydney looked at the outfit carefully. Then she looked at me.

"Perfect," pronounced Sydney.

"It's totally you, Cashmere!" Quinn squealed. "Payton, how'd you do it?"

By memorizing a zillion magazine tips and celebrity photos and tracking down trends online? Really, it had been just like cramming for any competition.

"Um, well, I just picked stuff that would highlight Cashmere's best features," I said. (And hide her flaws. I did not say that.)

"You so did it, Payton," said Sydney. "Now Cashmere

has her own look and won't need to borrow *my* clothes. Kidding!"

Yes! I so did it! Now, for the next round of the fashion bee . . .

"My turn!" Quinn ran into the cubicle to change into the outfit I'd picked for her.

"I simply pulled together pieces like ones she already had, with just a few edgier ones to update the look," I informed Sydney and Cashmere while we were waiting.

They stared at me. Whoops! I sounded like Emma when I said that! I'd better cover up.

"Um . . . like . . . when I go into my fashion forecasting . . . um . . . mode, I, like, get totally intense, you know?" I said. And forced out a giggle.

"Fashion *is* serious business." Sydney nodded.

Whew.

"Eeeee!" Quinn came out of the dressing room. "I looooove it!"

"I do too," Cashmere piped up. "And Quinn, you can wear it with the shoes you have, which is like thank goodness because"—she paused and looked at me-"Quinn's allowance is not all that. It's such a downer on our shopping trips."

I noticed Quinn's face fall for a second. Then she came over to me.

"Thanks, Payton." She smiled.

"Now get in there, Payton, and show us what you got," Sydney commanded.

I went into the cubicle and put on the outfit I'd picked out for myself. I came out and climbed up on the platform. Whoa . . . my moment in the glaring fluorescent lights. I saw five Paytons in the lit-up mirrors and felt a little dizzy.

And then I heard it.

The oohs. And ahhhs. The compliments. It was like a replay of the applause at the spelling bee, except this time my accomplishment was very different.

I know, I know. This was silly and superficial. But it was the first time since the start of middle school that people were actually paying attention to me.

"You are a genius," Sydney proclaimed.

A genius!

I posed in front of the mirrors and couldn't help smiling. *Oh. Yeah. I'm a supastar! The Number One Shopping Mall Champion! The Queen of the Fashion Bee!*

Take that, Jazmine James!

"I'll take it all," I told the salesperson a few minutes

later. We were all at the checkout. I took out my parents' credit card, which was to be used only in an emergency. Well, wasn't Payton always calling me a fashion emergency? I'd pay my parents back, of course. This would put a dent in my college savings fund, but I was on such a happy buzz I didn't care.

"There's a fifteen percent discount off all totals over a hundred dollars," the salesperson told me.

I calculated the savings in my head.

"That's nineteen dollars," I said automatically. Big oops. I looked around and saw Sydney and Cashmere walking away, loaded down with store bags. Pheee-ew. They hadn't heard me. But Quinn had.

"Payton," Quinn said to me. "You're like two different people sometimes."

Er. Um.

"Payton! Q! Come on!" Sydney called to us.

I took my pink and lime-green bags and followed Quinn out of the store. We joined Sydney and Cashmere.

Who were talking to some boys. And one of them was Ox.

"We're all going to the food court before my mom picks us up," Sydney announced, indicating the boys, too.

Suddenly my bags felt very heavy, and my legs felt wobbly.

"I got these," Ox said, taking my bags.

"What a gentleman," Sydney cooed to him. She shoved her bags at him too.

"Logan, carry my bags?" Cashmere said in a baby voice to some guy.

"No way—those bags are pink," he said. "You bought it, you carry it."

Cashmere's face turned as pink as her bags.

"Here." Ox took hers, too. "It's a good workout."

He held up the bags like he was lifting weights. I couldn't help but notice how his arm muscles looked strong and—

Okay.

Ox and I were walking side by side. I had no clue what to say.

"So, you like football?" I blurted out. Um. Duh-umb.

"It's cool," Ox said. "It's not what I'm planning to do for the rest of my life, but it's cool."

Wait. I thought jocks only wanted to talk about jock things. Like, "Football rules! Tackle and injure! Maim and bruise!"

"Oh," I said, brilliantly.

"Yeah, I'd really like to work for a wildlife organization and help protect animal habitats," Ox said. He sounded a little . . . shy? Could a popular football player be shy? It made me feel a little braver.

"You're really into animals, then," I said.

"Yeah, ever since my parents got me this animal encyclopedia for kids," Ox said, shifting the shopping bags around.

"Hey, I had that book too!" I exclaimed.

We walked to the food court in a group.

"Uh, thanks for holding my bags," I said, shyly.

"Remember, an ox is hardworking," he said.

"I know! Because an ox can carry heavy loads for long distances!" I said to him happily.

He smiled at me!

He had a nice smile. For a big jock person, I mean. Anyway.

So. I had about twenty minutes before Sydney's mother came. Twenty minutes to:

1. keep Sydney happy with me—
   I mean Payton.
2. make sure Payton was part of their group
   for when we switched back tomorrow.

3. spend a few remaining minutes with Ox
   before I had to change back into Emma.

And never talk to him again.

We were all in line at SuperSalads. The girls, I mean. The boys were off in the pizza line.

"One smoothie," I ordered, when it was my turn. Just like Sydney. And Cashmere. And Quinn.

We sat down at a round table. And . . .

Ox sat down next to me! He sat down next to me! Okay! Okay! He turned to talk to someone on his other side. I reached into Payton's tote and checked my teeth in the purse mirror. Clear. Okay.

But I also noticed Sydney looking at Ox. And looking at me. I realized there was an empty seat on her other side, and Ox had chosen the seat next to me.

"The salesperson said that Sydney looks like a model in her new outfit," I said, really loudly.

"She totally does." Cashmere's head bobbed up and down.

"You guys!" Sydney giggled. Yay. Happy Sydney = Happy Payton.

"You girls sure like to buy stuff," Ox said to me, eating his pizza slice.

"I know," I said.

"Girls and their stuff," he said, shaking his head like *What's that all about?*

"Maybe it's to cover up their insecurities," I said, thoughtfully. "Or for others, maybe it's just getting to be creative in a socially acceptable way. It *is* fascinating."

OMG.

Me and my (Emma's) big mouth. *That was so not something Payton would or should say! Now Ox is going to think I'm some geek or freak or . . .*

"Hey, Payton," Ox said.

"Um, yeah?" I asked him.

"I'm glad you came to the mall," Ox said. He smiled right at me.

Squee!!!

Nineteen

MONDAY, BACK HOME

"Thanks for the ride!" I called out to Nick's mom, as her minivan pulled out of my driveway.

I waved good-bye until the car pulled out of sight. Then I took off. I raced around to the back of the house as Emma's text message had instructed me to do.

"Payton?" my mom called out. "Emma? Is that you?"

Oh, my gosh.

"Hurry!" Emma's head stuck out from behind the garden shed. She waved me over frantically.

I jumped behind the tallest bush and quickly pulled off Emma's sweatshirt and sweatpants. I tossed them to her as she tossed me my (Summer Slave) hoodie and miniskirt and I pulled them on. Emma shoved my tote bag and some shopping bags at me and grabbed her own backpack.

Ouch! I got some pricker in my butt. Getting changed in the bushes of the backyard was not exactly my top choice, but it was too risky to try to get past Mom again.

"Wait!" Emma said. "Bracelets!"

I took off the *E* cuff and traded for the *P*.

"Okay, let's go!" I said. We ran around to the front of the house. And casually walked in the front door.

"Hi, Mom!" I said, cheerfully, although slightly out of breath.

"Hi, Mom!" Emma said, giving her a hug.

"How was your day, girls?" Mom asked. "Emma, how was your after-school club?"

Emma looked at me, questioning. I nodded and smiled.

"Superb!" she said.

"And how was the mall, Payton?" Mom asked me.

Emma gave me a thumbs-up behind Mom's back.

"Awesome!" I said.

"Mom, I have a ton of homework," Emma said. "So I'm going to get started."

"Me too," I said.

"Payton, I'm so pleased to see you focusing on your schoolwork," my mom said.

"Um, Emma's been a good influence on me," I said.

"Oh, no," Emma said modestly. "Payton's really become quite the student in middle school."

"And Emma," my mom exclaimed, "your hair is out of a ponytail! It looks nice!"

Oops, Emma had left her hair Paytonish.

"Payton's been a good influence on me, too," Emma said.

"Oh, you two! Give me a hug," Mom said, getting all emotional. "People always warn me that twins bicker and fight, but I tell them 'You should see my twins! They're always there for each other!'"

"Aw, that's so sweet," I said, giving my mom a hug. Then I raised my eyebrow at Emma like *Let's get out of here!*

"Homework time!" Emma said. And she linked arms with me and half dragged me up the stairs and into our room.

I pushed a pile of stuff off my bed and sat down on it. Emma sat down on her bed too.

"Okay, what happened? WHAT HAPPENED?" I squealed. "Where *were* you?"

"Me?" Emma shot back. "Where were *you*?"

"Well, I went to the school VOGS meeting!" I said.

"Oh, that's good! I wanted to join the Videocast of Gecko Students," Emma said. "Good work, Payton."

"Thank you!" I said, pleased. "And guess what? I volunteered you for the very first VOGS group!"

"I'm impressed," Emma said. "Did you carefully get my writing assignment?"

"Even better," I said, excitedly. "*You* are going to be a VOGS anchorwoman!"

"You mean anchor*person,*" Emma corrected me. "Wait a minute. What are you talking about?"

"You're an anchorperson!" I told her. "Only four people got picked and I—I mean *you*—are one of them! Jazmine James is too, and you should have seen her face when they announced your name. It was classic! You get to write your own story! You love writing! And then, you get to read it on air! On the school news!"

"Are you kidding?" Emma asked.

"I know, isn't it awesome?" I bounced on her bed with excitement. "You know how you said you wanted to stop being invisible in middle school? Now everyone will know you! You will be the face of the video news!"

I sat back on my bed and waited for her to thank me and tell me that I was the best twin ever!

"Payton! How could you do that to me?" Emma wailed.

That didn't sound like a thank-you.

"Um," I said. "I thought you'd want to?"

"You know me and videos! I'll choke! I'll panic! I'll look like an idiot! People will think I'm stupid!" Emma wailed.

Oh. Uh-oh. That's right. Emma could stand up in front of a lot of people in her bees, but she hated to be on video. She never even let my parents film her competitions in case she looked stupid, she said.

"Um," I said. "I thought it would be cool. I, um, did a practice round, and it was kind of fun."

We'd done a fake broadcast. I'd done a pretend news story where I talked about how gross the school lunches were—like, say, the oozy burritos. Hee. And I discussed the need for better nutrition and healthy, good-tasting options. People clapped for me and everything.

"Well," Emma said with a sigh, "I'll just have to tell Mrs. Burkle tomorrow to choose somebody else."

"Uh," I said. "Actually, you go to rehearsal tomorrow. You're going to be an anchor."

"Tomorrow? Absolutely not," Emma said. "Now I have to e-mail Mrs. Burkle and ask her to pick someone else. I can't believe you did that."

"Um . . . and there's also a pep rally instead of ninth period tomorrow," I told her. "Where the whole school goes to an assembly and watches . . . a live broadcast of VOGS."

"Wait—WHAT???" Emma started pretty much freaking out. "No! It's not possible! I've got to contact Mrs. Burkle!"

She got up to go to the computer.

"Calm down, Emma," I said. "Breathe."

Emma shrieked instead. "My e-mail is down! Oh, no!"

"I'm sorry!" I said. "I got caught up being . . ."

Being Emma, I guess.

People had called me smart two times that day. I couldn't remember the last time anyone had told me I was smart. I'd . . . kind of liked it. Plus, I couldn't have let that Jazmine James win a spot if Emma didn't. Wow, was I getting competitive like Emma? Wait! What was Emma doing when I was being her?

"So then where were *you* all this time?" I asked Emma.

"At the mall with Sydney and company," Emma said, sitting down on her bed and taking a deep breath.

"What?! WHAT?" I screamed. "How did *that* happen?"

"Well, I told you I'd fix things for you," Emma said, modestly. "All in a day's work."

"Wait." I got worried. "Are you sure they didn't ask you to make fun of you or anything?"

"Does *this* sound like they're making fun of me?" Emma handed me her cell phone—my cell phone—and showed me two text messages:

Luuuuuv my new clothes cu at lunch! Q

"*Q* stands for Quinn," Emma informed me.

I'd figured that out. I was busy scrolling through to read the next text message.

Tooo much fun. Mall again this weekend? xoxox Syd

"AHHHH!" I screamed. "You not only made up with Sydney, but she's inviting you to the mall *and* saying you were fun?! YOU?"

"It's true," Emma said. "I was fun. And, dare I say . . . cool."

"Whoa," I said. "Unreal."

I watched Emma as she took some lip gloss out of my tote bag and expertly put some on her lips.

"Ahem. And now you're putting on lip gloss," I pointed out.

"Oh," Emma said. "Habit, I guess. Plus, this peach mango flavor is kind of tasty."

"Um, that's my lip gloss from my tote bag," I pointed out. "May I have it back?"

"Fine," Emma sighed, handing it over. "I bought my own cherry cola flavor at the mall anyway. So, in sum, this was a successful experiment. You are so in with Sydney. You can go back to being you without any more burrito embarrassment."

"And you have experienced being popular and having friends," I said. "So, now we can go back to being ourselves."

I flopped back on my bed and looked at the ceiling. Emma was lying on her bed too.

"Emma?" I said. "I know this is a dumb question but . . . you *do* want to switch back, right?"

Emma didn't answer. She just chewed on her hair.

And then my cell phone rang. I rolled over on my bed and looked at the caller ID. I didn't recognize the number.

"Hello?" I said.

"Payton?" a guy's deep voice said. "Hey, it's Ox."

Ox? The burrito guy?

I muted the phone.

"It's the guy I spilled the burrito on!" I said to Emma.

"Ox?" she said. And then her eyes got all huge. "Ox is calling you? I mean me?"

"He's calling you?" I was confused. "Why? For homework help? But he's not in any of your classes . . ."

I handed her the phone.

"What do I say?" she asked me, frantically. And then I saw her turning purple.

"Put him on speaker!" I said.

"Sorry, Ox," Emma stammered. "I'm here."

Ox's voice boomed loudly over the speaker-phone.

"Hey, Payton," Ox said. "Tomorrow's the pep rally. The football players have to sit near the front, 'cause, you know. Everyone cheers us on or whatever."

Emma looked at me. I shrugged back at her.

"Well," Ox continued, "if you want, I can save a seat for you."

"But I'm not a football player," Emma said back.

"I figured that out," said Ox. "But friends sit with us, and I . . . dunno. I just thought I could save you a seat or something."

Emma's eyes got wide. And that's when I realized it.

EMMA HAD A CRUSH!

And even more major:

EMMA HAD A CRUSH WHO CALLED HER!

AND WHO ASKED HER TO SIT WITH HIM AT THE PEP RALLY!

!!!!

Emma muted the phone again.

"Did he just ask me to sit next to him at the pep rally?" Emma asked me.

"Yes!" I said. "Well, he asked me. But really, he wants to sit by you! Pretending to be me!"

"I get it, I get it!" Emma cut me off. "So what do I say?"

I looked at her, sitting there, all nervous.

"You say *yes*."

Emma unmuted the phone and said, "Yes."

"Cool. See you tomorrow at lunch," Ox said, and hung up.

"EMMA MILLS!" I screamed. "A BOY JUST CALLED YOU! And asked to sit next to you! In public!!!"

I saw her blush. I'd never seen her like this before!

"You liiiike him," I sang. "Emma and Ox! Sitting in a tree! This is so major! I never would have thought you would like a big football jock guy!"

"Oh, be quiet," Emma said, but she was grinning. "He's actually more than just a football guy. Did you know he wants to work protecting animal habitats? This is phenomenal! No, wait . . . this is disastrous!"

Emma wasn't smiling any more.

"Disastrous?" I said. "How is it disastrous? You have a sort-of date at the pep rally!"

"No," Emma said. "*You* have a sort of date. Think about it. Tomorrow, I'm back to being me."

Oh.

That.

"Oh," I said. "You're right."

Emma lay down on her bed again and chewed her hair.

"Payton," she said. "I kind of . . . well, it's just that . . . he's cute and interesting. I mean, I know that after he hangs out with me a little more he won't like me, but . . . I wish I could just go to the pep rally and sit near Ox!"

She really was crushing on this guy!

"Of *course* you have to go with him tomorrow. Whatever it takes, we will make it happen. Whatever it takes."

"Well, we could switch for the pep rally," Emma said.

Which would be perfect! Because while Emma was being me at the pep rally, I could go be her at VOGS!

That *was* perfect! Because I'd had fun being the VOGS news anchor. But it was only for honors students, so I'd never get a chance to do it as myself.

I opened my mouth to tell Emma that.

"Pleeeease let me be you again," Emma begged. "Just to see Ox. I owe you big time."

I was about to tell her she didn't owe me anything, but I kept quiet. I'd never seen Emma so desperate.

"Okay, here's an offer you can't refuse," she said. Emma went over to the side of the room and picked up some shopping bags.

"If you let me be you, all these will be yours!"

Emma reached in and pulled out some way cute

clothes that had tags on them. She spread them out on my bed.

"Whoa! These are sweeet!" I said. Sydney must have really given her some good fashion advice. They were so un-Emma. They were so *me*. Maybe Sydney or Quinn had helped her pick them out.

"I can have them?" I asked.

"If you let me wear them first to the pep rally with Ox," Emma said.

"Emma," I said. "Toss in this pair of sweats for me to study in tonight, and you have a deal."

"Deal," Emma said, solemnly. "I promise to be the best Payton I can be for one more day."

"And I promise to be Emmarrific for one more day," I said.

Emma stuck out her pinky and so did I. We linked them.

"TWIN-ky swear!!!"

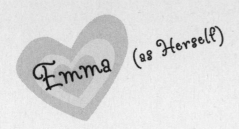
Emma *(as Herself)*

Twenty

TUESDAY MORNING

I made a chart, copied it, and gave one copy to Payton.

"Remember, do not lose this paper," I told Payton, as we stood at our lockers.

"Duh." Payton rolled her eyes. "I've got the paper. Don't start stressing. You've got everything planned perfectly."

True.

The homeroom warning bell rang. I walked to my own homeroom. I was starting the day as myself.

"Bye, PAYTON!" I said.

"Bye, EMMA!" My sister waved and went off to homeroom. Boy, those clothes looked cute on her. I'd picked out:

☑ a blue sweater
☑ a blue and white cami
☑ a gray cami under that
☑ a cute skirt

Her outfit was extra important, because I'd be the one wearing it when I saw Ox. We'd decided not to switch places all day. Just at a few key times. I'd made up the schedule.

```
Period
H        P=P              E=E
1        P=P              E=E
2        P=P              E=E
3        P=P              E=E
4        P=P              E=E

JC*

5        P=E              E=P
6        P=P              E=E

JC*

7        P=E              E=P
8        P=E              E=P
9  (assembly!!!)
         P=E              E=P

JC*
```

"This looks like math," Payton had complained when I first gave her the schedule.

"Well, it is similar to algebra, where variables repre-sent —," I mused.

"Emma!" she'd said.

Okay, okay. We'd start the day as ourselves. And be ourselves all the way through fourth period.

"And then we'll meet at the janitor's closet, the JC, to trade places. So fifth period I get to be Payton. And have lunch at the same time as . . . well, you know."

I felt my face turn purple.

"With your boyfriend," Payton sang. "Your BF, your true love . . ."

"Ahem. Continuing on," I said. "It's back to our-selves for sixth period. You'll go to your own English with Mrs. Burkle. Then the big switch is for seventh and eighth periods and last-period assembly."

"Yeah, because I've got VOGS rehearsal seventh period," Payton said. "So I've got to be you."

"And we'll stay switched until dismissal, when we'll quickly flip back and go home," I finished.

It really wasn't that complicated. And it was just for one last day. Then everything would be back to normal. I'd be regular Emma. For the rest of my life . . . well, I wouldn't think about that now. One period at a time.

Starting with homeroom. Which was kind of weird, because people I didn't know said, "Hi, Emma."

"Er, hello," I mumbled as I lugged my backpack to my seat. Sheesh, was it always this heavy? I opened my vocabulary study book.

Loquacious: talkative

"Hey, Emma," a boy said.

"Oh, hey," I said. It was the boy who sat behind me. I looked back at my vocabulary word, but something really strange happened. The boy kept talking, something about VOGS and reporting techniques and . . .

"Uh huh, yeah." I kept nodding like I knew what he was talking about.

"You were great yesterday," he said.

I was? I mean, Payton was?

"So were you," I said.

"Uh, great at what?" he asked me.

Oh. Uh . . .

"Just great in general!" I managed.

He gave me a weird look, but fortunately, the teacher started taking attendance.

I bolted before he could say anything else. It was a relief when I could get to Science. Where everything would be normal.

Dr. Perkins told the class to pair up for an experiment on density.

"Jazmine," she said, "please help Ahmad today." Ahmad was wearing an arm cast and sling. He moved beside Jazmine. Everyone was moving toward their friends. I sat. And waited. Hoping there'd be someone who needed a partner.

But no. There was an odd number of students today. I was left the odd one out.

"Emma, psst," I heard someone say.

Huh? Tess and Hector were waving me over to where they were setting up their little metal masses.

"Okay," I said, joining them. *They must either feel sorry for me or want to use my science brain.* I was used to both.

"Emma, Hector and I were talking about what you said in math yesterday," Tess said. "You were so right. It's why I don't join after-school clubs unless Jazmine and Hecky are there to protect me."

"Yeah, I felt like that the time I went to band camp and was the only one who brought my instrument to the

Saturday night dance," Hector said. "What a faux pas! I couldn't even hide it, because it was my harp!"

Tess burst into giggles. I was completely lost. What the heck was going on here? Why were these virtual strangers—friends of Jazmine James—confessing their embarrassing moments to me?

I started moving the little metal weights onto the measuring scale.

"Density," I said, changing the subject to classwork, where at least I would have a clue. "How thick an object is. How much mass it displaces."

"She's right," Hector said. "Time to focus."

"It's funny, Emma," Tess said. "Sometimes it seems like you're two different people."

"It does," Jazmine said, coming over from the table next to us. She looked at me thoughtfully. "It does seem like you're two different people sometimes."

"Er," I said. *Change of subject! Change of subject!*

"Density!" I said, picking up the mass. "Ten grams. So, how many fluid ounces will it displace?"

Luckily, just then Ahmad knocked over their scale with his cast. Jazmine hurried back to her partner.

We went to work on the science experiment. On the outside I was focused. But inside? I was counting down the minutes to fifth period. When I would see Ox. In Payton's lunch period.

But first I had three more classes to get through. I had thought it would be a relief to be my comfy Emma self, but nothing was making any sense.

"Do you really think they'll improve the lunches?" a girl with braids and a baggy sweater asked me in Social Studies. "I liked what you said at VOGS about better nutrition and better taste making better students."

Um, thanks?

Then, a little later . . .

"Awesome speech in Math yesterday!" some boy said, giving me a thumbs-up in the hall.

What the heck did Payton do in Math?

The most bizarre moments came during lunch. I was sitting with Tess, Hector, and Jazmine. I'd pulled out my language arts novel and pretended to be riveted by it, so no one would interrupt. (And ask me about music lessons.)

First, Hector couldn't get his chip bag open.

"It's okay to ask for help," Tess told him. "Right, Emma?"

I looked up, and she winked at me. Wha—?

"Jazmine, would you please, please help me?" Hector said, dramatically. "I need your help, Jazmine. But then, we all need a little help sometimes—right, Emma?"

"Right?" I agreed. What the heck?

Jazmine James did not look amused. She took one long slurp of her smoothie. Then she glared at me.

"Never mind; I got it open." Hector dug into his chip bag, and I went back to my book.

Jazmine took another long, loud slurp of smoothie.

"Ladies do not make noises while eating," boomed a loud voice.

I looked up from my book. And looked even farther up. A very tall woman with short dark hair stood over our table. Whoa. Her face was the grown-up version of Jazmine's face. And this woman's face was not smiling.

"Hi, Mama," Jazmine said.

"Is that the way you show respect? Stand up and greet me properly," Jazmine's mother said.

Jazmine rolled her eyes and stood up. People at other tables had quieted down and were watching.

"I'm here to see that your middle school is running smoothly," Jazmine's mother said. "I've already met with a few of your teachers and reminded them of our family's high standards and expectations of excellence."

"Hello, Mrs. James!" Hector jumped up.

"Nice to see you, Mrs. James." Tess stood up too.

"Hector, Tess, darlings!" Mrs. James nodded. "And who is this?"

Jazmine's mother looked at me. Yikes. Her eyes were like laser beams.

"Mama, this is Emma Mills," Jazmine didn't seem too enthused to introduce me. Mrs. James looked even less pleased.

"And what brings you to my Jazmine's lunch table?" Mrs. James asked me.

Uh . . . desperation?

"Emma won the state spelling bee last year," Tess offered.

"Ah, yes, I believe I've met your father," Mrs. James said. "Talkative man. And I'm sure you'll be a gracious runner-up when my Jazmine wins this year."

With that, she spun around and started to walk away.

"Good-bye, children," she said over her shoulder. "I have an appointment with the principal. Study hard! Strive for perfection!"

And she was gone.

Our table was quiet. Whoa. Now I knew where Jazmine got her personality. I almost felt sorry for her, having a mother like that. At least my own parents never pushed me or pressured me. Or hunted me down in the cafeteria.

Hector looked around at the people still looking at us.

"The show is over, people," Hector announced loudly. "There's nothing to see here."

"I need to stop at the library before next class," Jazmine said, gathering her things. "Bye, Hector. Bye, Tess."

Jazmine spun around, just like her mother had, and left.

Oookay. I'd been dissed. I didn't feel sorry for that girl anymore. Can you spell n-a-s-t-y?

"Emma, I—" Tess started to say something.

Clang! Clang! The bell drowned out the rest of Tess's sentence. Whatever. Any friend of Jazmine's is no friend of mine.

I wouldn't think about Tess, Hector, or Jazmine right now. There was no time to waste. I had more important things to do. I was off to meet Payton.

Payton (about to be Emma)

Twenty-one

BETWEEN FOURTH AND FIFTH PERIODS

Knock. Knock-tap-tap. Knock!

I knocked our secret code on the janitor's closet.

"Payton?" Emma opened the door a crack.

"Payton about to be Emma!" I whispered back cheerfully. "Open up!"

The door opened and a hand pulled me inside. I turned my locker mirror light on, shining it on Emma's face. Oops.

Emma stood there looking at me accusingly.

"What the heck did you do?" she asked me.

"Um," I said. "I'm not sure?"

"Why are people talking to me in my classes?" Emma demanded.

"Oh, that!" I said. "Well, I said hi to people."

"What else did you say?" Emma said. "I thought you were supposed to have otolaryngitis and not speak?"

"Well, excuse me," I said. "I thought I'd perk up your social life. Make you a little approachable."

"A *little* approachable?" Emma said. "Tess and Hector were telling me every awkward moment they've ever had! Like we're all close friends, sharing deep secrets. And I'm practically being mauled by people high-fiving me over some non-answer you apparently gave in math class . . . ?"

Oh. That. Um, yeah.

Clang!

The warning bell for class!

"No time to talk!" I said. "We have to switch!"

And the first switch of the day was on! Clothes were tossed back and forth!

Lip gloss put on; lip gloss wiped off! Hair up; hair down! Bags handed over!

And . . .

Ta-da!

And . . .

Clang!

"I need answers later," Emma said. "This morning was very confusing to me. And you know I don't like being confused."

"Gotta run!" I said, before she had time to grill me any more. "Good luck, Payton-Emma!"

I opened the door and walked very casually out. Two seconds later Emma followed.

I went left down the hall. She went right.

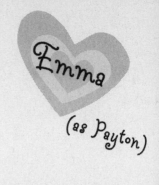
Emma
(as Payton)

Twenty-two

LUNCH

I went right to the lunchroom. I was nervous. And excited. I was about to see Ox! And spend one more day sitting at the popular table.

Did I just think that? Incredibly shallow of me, I know. But maybe I could soak up some more compliments about my incredible fashion skills and do a little girly bonding with my peeps.

Is "peeps" a kewl word? Maybe not. Anyway, I walked into the lunchroom. Smiley. Cheery. And Paytony.

I slid into my seat next to Sydney, Cashmere, and Quinn.

"Hey, guys," I said. I noticed that Sydney was wearing

the necklace I'd picked out for her at the mall.

"Hi, Payton," Quinn said. "The shirt looks so cute on you!"

"Thanks!" I said. "And that necklace I picked out looks so cute on you! And Sydney, I love your shirt."

"Don't the earrings I picked out for Sydney look so cute too?" Cashmere asked.

"Sure," I said. "Although I found this pair in a magazine I have got to show you, Syd."

"Ooh, I can't wait," Sydney said. "Let's go shopping again. How about after school Thursday?"

"I've got jazz and tap on Thursday," Cashmere whined.

"Oh, well. You'll have to come next time, Cashmere." Sydney dismissed her. I did catch the dirty look Cashmere gave me.

"So. Is Thursday good for you, Payton?" Sydney asked me.

Well, actually, not really. I'll have a mathletics meeting. And also, I won't be Payton.

I focused intently on eating my turkey wrap.

"Let's go shopping Thursday," Sydney said. "Bring your credit card; we're doing some serious damage, Payton. I saw this coat that's so you—it's a hundred and fifty bucks, but so worth it."

A hundred and fifty dollars? Didn't I just have a spending spree that blew out my savings? Wasn't that enough?

"And you need new jewelry," Cashmere said. "That *P* cuff is growing old."

"Definitely," Sydney said. "That cuff has to go."

I twirled the *P* cuff around my wrist. This lunch wasn't as fun as I'd expected. I hoped something good would happen.

Ooh! And here it was. Ox was walking into the cafeteria.

Ox!

And he saw me, and he waved and smiled at me.

Ox waved and smiled at me!

I smiled and started to wave back. Sydney waved, too.

"That Ox," Sydney said. "He's so quiet, but who cares with those football muscles."

Mmm. *So true,* I thought.

"Did you see him wave at me?" Sydney said. "He totally likes me."

I nearly choked on my turkey wrap.

"You guys would make the cutest couple!" Cashmere squealed. "You could go to the football games and cheer him on from the stands and it would be so romantic."

"Finally!" Quinn said. "Ox has never paid any attention to any girls."

Uh.

"I don't know," I said weakly. "I think you and Cameron look so good together."

"Cameron and Noah are kind of juvenile compared to Ox," Sydney said. "Ox is so . . . mature."

"Sydney, he's coming over!" Cashmere squealed.

"Watch me work my magic," Sydney said, swiping on some lip gloss. "Watch and learn, girls. Watch and learn."

Uh.

Uh.

What do I do? What would Payton do?

I looked down and busied myself unwrapping a pack of cheese crackers. Maybe Ox would just pass by, and then Sydney would forget about him and move on to one of her other gajillion guys, and I could catch him later and—

"Hey," Ox came right up to our table.

"Hi, Ox!" Sydney said, all flirty.

"Hey, guys," Ox said. "Hey, Payton."

"Hey!" I squeaked.

He looked at me and smiled. I smiled weakly back. Man, he was so cute. His blue shirt made his eyes stand out and—

"I'm sooo psyched for the pep rally today!" Sydney said to him.

"Yeah, me too," said Ox. "Hey, Payton. Still up for today?"

Uh.

"Up for what?" Sydney asked.

"Meeting me at the pep rally," Ox said. "Payton? You still want to?"

Uh.

I so still wanted to. But I caught the look on Sydney's face. This was too much pressure for me.

"Glah!" I said to him.

Yes, I said "glah." I choked, okay?

He gave me a funny look.

"Ox! Dude! Get over here!" Some guys were calling him over to their table.

"Well, see ya at the pep rally," Ox said.

I watched him walk to his lunch table. Then I turned to face the six eyes staring at me.

"Payton. Is there something you'd like to tell us?" Sydney said.

I looked up at her. She looked pleasant, but Quinn and Cashmere were staring down at the table.

"Like, what's up with you and Ox?" Sydney asked me.

"Uh," I said. "I don't know. He sort of asked me if I wanted to sit with them at the pep rally."

"Eee!" Quinn said. "He's saving you a seat with the football players? That's so major!"

"And you weren't going to tell your very best friends about this?" Sydney said. "Especially, for example, when one of them—*me*—was saying how she might consider going out with him?"

Uh.

"I wasn't sure how to—," I stammered. "I didn't know what to—"

"Payton, I can't believe you're stealing Sydney's crush!" Cashmere said. "I mean, she told you she liked him. She's even giving up Cameron and Justin for him!"

"I wasn't stealing anyone's crush!" I said. "I didn't know Sydney might like him, and—"

"Well, now you do," Sydney said to me.

I looked over at Ox. He looked up and smiled at me again.

"You're not going to sit with him at the pep rally, are you?" Cashmere asked me.

Uh.

"Then it's settled," Sydney said. She waved and smiled at Ox.

"Once Ox knows he has a chance with Sydney, it would be all over with you anyway, Payton," Cashmere whispered to me under her breath.

"So now I totally need those sneakers ASAP, Payton," Sydney said to me.

"Sneakers?" I stammered.

"Duh, my CocoBella sneakers," Sydney said.

Uh. Oh. Those sneakers. I'd forgotten about that. Apparently she hadn't.

"You *can* get those sneakers—right, Payton?" Cashmere looked at me slyly.

Uh.

"They'll look perfect when I'm cheering on Ox at the game," Sydney said.

"Oh, look at that!" I exclaimed, pulling out Payton's cell phone. "I have a text message! Oh! I have a meeting with a teacher! Gotta go!"

"I didn't even hear it vibrate," Cashmere said suspiciously.

"Bye!" I jumped up and grabbed my lunch tray. And . . .

I was wearing Payton's (Summer Slave) platform shoes, and I . . .

Oh, no. I tripped. The remains of my turkey wrap,

crackers, and soda spilled off my tray and . . . didn't land on Sydney. No, they didn't land on Ox.

They landed on the floor. Which meant I slipped on them.

And I landed on the floor too.

Crunch. The cute skirt was now splotched on the rear. I jumped up and thought fast. I tugged the blue sweater down in the back, grabbed Payton's backpack, tossed my tray on the dirty dish counter, and rushed out of the lunchroom.

I didn't look back.

Payton
(as Emma)

Twenty-three

AFTER SIXTH PERIOD

Knock. Knock-tap-tap. Knock!

"Just get in here!" Emma opened the door and practically dragged me in.

"I need your help," Emma said. "Things have gotten out of control."

Out of control? In only one period? We'd already switched one more time last period and all had been totally fine.

Emma started babbling. "I have to go shopping for new clothes and a hundred-and-fifty-dollar jacket and you have to get more Summer Slave sneakers but they're not even out yet and that's not even the major thing. She likes Ox! SHE LIKES OX!!!"

Oh. Kay. Clearly my twin sister had lost her mind.

"Too much pressure," Emma cried. "Too much social pressure!"

"Emma!" I shook her shoulders. "Get a grip! Take a deep breath!"

Emma took a deep breath.

"You're right," she said. "Where have my priorities gone? I'm a champion debater, for gosh sakes. Okay. I've made my decision. I can't go to the pep rally."

"What?" I said.

"I have to give up," Emma said. "My little crush on some jock is not worth messing things up for you."

"I don't care if you go out with a jock," I assured her. "In fact, I think it's cool. Hey, does he play basketball? Maybe you'll even want to try out for basketball cheerleading with me!"

"Are you insane?" Emma asked. "No, what I mean was, I have to give up. Sydney likes Ox; thus, I cannot."

"Really?" I said. "You're giving up your crush because of Sydney?"

"Payton, your friendships with people are more important than some . . . silly . . . crush. I can't risk Sydney being mad at you all over again just because I like Ox. You and your happiness are more important to me."

Wow. Emma was giving up that for . . . me? For my happiness?

"Wow!" I threw my arms around her. "Emma, you are the best!"

"Yeah." Emma sighed. She looked sad. "I know."

"So, we're not trading places?" I asked her.

"No, you still have to do VOGS," Emma said. "I've had enough trauma for one day. I'll just hide out in the library during the assembly so I don't have to deal with Ox."

Phew. I was hoping she'd say that. I'd been kind of excited about VOGS all day.

"Okay, then," she said. "Let's switch."

Clothes were tossed back and forth! Lip gloss put on; lip gloss wiped off! Hair up; hair down! Cuffs traded; bags handed over!

"I'm ready," I told Emma. It took her a little longer to get ready, since she had to do her hair and put on lip gloss. "Wish me luck."

"Good luck," Emma said. "Wait! Don't forget your schedule."

She held the switching schedule out to me. I opened

the door and casually stepped out of the janitor's closet and—

OOF!

Right into Jazmine James! Our backpacks fell off and papers flew everywhere.

"Oh!" I said. "Um! I'm so sorry!"

"Ouch!" Jazmine said. "Did you just attack me? Is this sabotage, Emma? Are you trying to keep me from anchoring VOGS out of jealousy and a justified fear that I am better than you?"

"What? No!" I said. "I'm not trying to attack you! I just . . . fell."

Jazmine looked around.

"You fell out of the janitor's closet?" she asked me.

"Um," I tried to think of an excuse. "Yes. Yes I did. I was spacing out and went in there thinking it was the bathroom."

I leaned down to pick up our stuff, which was all over the floor. I handed some of Jazmine's papers and notebooks back to her. She scooped up the remaining papers and looked through them.

"These are yours," she said, giving me a couple. "And these are mine."

Jazmine was putting the papers in her backpack

when I heard a creak.

And then the door to the janitor's closet started to open.

Oh, no! Emma was about to come out! There's no way Jazmine would believe both of us twins would have accidentally thought the janitor's closet was a bathroom!

I leaned against the door.

"So! Jazmine!" I said loudly, hoping Emma would hear me. "What's new, JAZMINE? JAZMINE JAMES?"

The janitor's closet door started opening again. Obviously, she couldn't hear me. I leaned against it with all my strength.

"Stay! Stay!" I hissed into the crack in the door.

"Are you talking to yourself?" Jazmine asked. "You know, I heard you were going to be competition for me in the brains department. But frankly, I'm not feeling too threatened, Emma."

Jazmine shook her head and walked down the hall.

I waited until she was out of sight, and opened the door.

"Coast is clear," I said. "Let's go."

Emma stepped out casually, looking all Payton.

"Hi!" she said brightly. I decided not to tell her

about the run-in with Jazmine. We had more important things to do right then, like make it to class on time. And I didn't want to be late. Because while Emma was off to my math class (yawn), I was off to VOGS rehearsal! Yes! I was so excited! I walked into the VOGS classroom and immediately changed my mind.

Yesterday it was a regular classroom with desks and chairs. Today it looked totally like a real news studio.

"Do you like it?" Nick from Emma's homeroom pointed to the set. "I'm on tech crew. We worked on it all day."

"It looks like a real studio," I said. "It makes me nervous."

"No way," he said. "You'll be great."

"Thanks," I said. I took a deep breath and tried to relax.

"People!" Mrs. Burkle clapped her hands for our attention. "This is our dress rehearsal! No more mamby-pamby! Places, everyone!"

I stood offstage and watched as Jazmine James took her spot at the anchor desk. I was feeling pretty nervous.

"Five . . . four . . . three . . . two . . ."

"Good afternoon, Geckos!" Jazmine said. "Welcome to the first VOGS, by students, for students. And what better day to have it on than the day of our first pep rally?"

She paused.

"Mrs. Burkle? Who wrote this? I think there are lots of better ways to start than with a stupid pep rally. How about a geometry competition day, for example? I'd rock that. I went to math camp, and—"

"Jazmine," Mrs. Burkle said, "while I appreciate your input, it is a little late to offer these suggestions. The principal would like to begin the show with this. And since the principal has finally allowed me to do this VOGS project, please humor me."

Jazmine rolled her eyes.

"Fine," she said. Then she spoke in a monotone, reading right off the prepared PowerPoint. "Show your school spirit by cheering on our football team tonight. Captain Ox Garrett says the players are out to finally beat our rivals, the Raiders. Rah. Go, team. And all that."

Jazmine rolled her eyes.

"You're up next!" Nick whispered to me. He pointed to an empty seat next to Jazmine.

I took a deep breath and joined Jazmine at the desk.

"And for our next report, here's Emma Mills."

The camera turned to me. I could see my face in the

monitor. I stared back at myself, in Emma's ponytail and her clothes. It was weird to see the name EMMA MILLS on the screen underneath my face. I wanted to make her proud.

Here goes.

"Thanks, Jazmine," I said, my voice shaking a little. I had written my report myself. Emma was going to edit it, but she'd ended up doing her math homework until bedtime. So it was all me. I hoped it was okay.

"Hi, I'm Emma Mills," I said. "With a special report."

I had practiced my report so much, I had it practically memorized. It felt like it just flowed out of my mouth. I forgot that people were watching me. I forgot everything, except for the words I wanted to share with my audience.

It felt like I'd barely started when suddenly I was saying, "And now back to you, Jazmine."

I waited a second until I saw the camera had moved away.

Whew! I hadn't screwed up! I did it!

I saw Nick give me a thumbs-up. I grinned.

"Emma, that was simply marvelous! Glorious! Stupendous!" Mrs. Burkle said. "You make our honors program proud."

I made the honors program proud? Me? Payton Mills, who could barely make the low achievers proud?

"Really?" I asked.

"You have a nice way of connecting with the audience," she said.

"How about me?" Jazmine James came up to Mrs. Burkle.

"A little constructive criticism," Mrs. Burkle said to her. "If you could show a little more enthusiasm for the pep rally, that would be appropriate."

Jazmine frowned.

I, however, had no criticism, constructive or otherwise! I did great work! I made the honors program proud!

Yeeeeesssss!

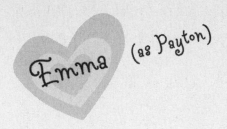
Emma (as Payton)

Twenty-four

NINTH PERIOD, PEP RALLY

"Honors passes are only for honors students," the librarian told me.

"But I *am* . . ." Oh, wait. *I'm not Emma. I'm Payton, who is NOT in Honors and canNOT get a pass to go to the library.*

"You need to go to the assembly, or I will have to report you." The librarian looked at me. It was a different librarian this time. More no-nonsense. This was so unfair. What? Just because I wasn't in honors, I wasn't allowed to go to the library? Wasn't reading one of the basics of education?

"Go," the librarian ordered, getting back to arranging a stack of books.

Guess not. Guess pep rallies took priority over literature.

I looked down to check the time. Oh, that's right, I wasn't wearing a watch. I was wearing my twin cuff. The one that was supposed to say *E* for "Emma" this period. But instead it said *P*.

I slunk through the halls toward the gym. I walked in.

Holey kamoley. The place was a zoo. People everywhere. I stayed against the back wall, trying to scope out a hiding place. I recognized Payton's PE teacher waving a giant green foam finger around. She pointed at our side of the gym. And then everyone screamed.

"GECK!" my half of the gym screamed.

"O!" the other half shouted back.

"GECK! O!"

Gack.

I watched as the gecko-costumed mascot danced around. Well, at least everyone's attention was focused on the gecko, and not on the geek looking around for a seat. That would be me—or at least it would be as soon as this period was over and I morphed back into my usual geeky Emma self.

Sigh.

"YOU!" Payton's PE teacher suddenly appeared

and yelled in my face. "Mills! Where's your spirit?"

The PE teacher shoved a giant green foam finger at me. I took it, not sure what I was supposed to do with it.

Tweeeet! The PE teacher blew her whistle at me. Okay, so much for inconspicuous. With all this yelling and whistling, half the crowd turned to look.

"GECK!" he yelled.

"O," I said. I waved the foam finger weakly.

"There's the spirit, Mills!" the PE teacher yelled. I pointed at the crowd. "Geck!" they shrieked. I spotted Margaret from the spelling bee standing up on her seat cheering. Boy, she was short. And Ahmad was raising his cast. I pointed at him. "O!" he and all the others yelled.

Oh, this was fun. Someone, get me out of this misery. Fortunately, Quinn and Cashmere spotted me.

"Payton!" Quinn yelled. "We saved you a seat!"

She pointed to a spot next to her on the bleachers.

I bolted in their direction to get away from Coach Hoen. I walked very carefully up the bleachers in my (Payton's? Ashlynn's?) platform shoes.

I slid into the seat next to Quinn.

"Where's Sydney?" I asked her.

She pointed to the front of the gym. And that's when I saw them.

Front row center. Sydney and Ox, sitting next to each other. Sydney was doing a hair-flippy thing and giggling. Ox was looking . . . hot.

Sigh. Well, that's the way it goes in Popular World. What Queen Bee wants, Queen Bee gets. Just like Jazmine James, Queen Bee of the Academic World.

And that's when the giant green gecko mascot headed up the bleachers. And toward me. I moved to the side to let it through, but it stopped at me. And pointed at me.

"You've got the green gecko finger, Payton!" Quinn squealed. "Lead the cheer!"

Oh, you have got to be kidding me.

I give up. I absolutely, totally give up.

I stood up on the bleacher. I held up the stupid giant foam finger and pointed at the other side of the gym.

"GECK!" they screamed.

Then I pointed at our side.

"O!"

"GECK!"

"Hey, Payton!" I looked up. That wasn't part of the cheer. It was Ox, yelling over the crowd and pointing at me and waving at me to come over to him.

I would just pretend not to see him. I led the crowd in another round of the cheer.

"GECK!"

Oh! Ox was making his way across the gym, toward the bleachers, and—

"Hey, Payton!" he yelled. "Come on!"

"Why is Ox calling *you*?" Cashmere said.

"Go talk to him," Quinn said. "I'll take over the gecko finger."

Ox was looking at me. And looking cute. Well. I had no choice.

I handed Quinn the foam finger, and she started waving it. I walked carefully down the bleachers, step by step. I glanced up to see Quinn dancing around with the foam finger as everyone around me GECKed and Oed.

"I was looking for you!" Ox said. "I got you a seat!"

I followed him down to the first row, front and center. I tried to avoid catching Sydney's eye as she glared at me. Um. There was no open seat. They were full of football players and cheerleader types.

"Sydney," Ox said. "I found Payton! Okay, she needs her seat."

I froze. Sydney froze.

"Her seat?" Sydney asked.

"Yeah, I told her I was saving a seat for her," Ox said. "So, now that I told you about the math homework, do you have any other questions for me?"

Sydney's eyes narrowed.

How awesome would it be, sitting next to Ox front row center at the pep rally? Cheering him on!

But hello. Reality check. I had to save Payton's friendship with Sydney.

Just then my cell phone rang. *Twinkle, twinkle, little star . . .*

Sydney snorted.

"That's your new ringtone, Payton? Isn't that a little juvenile? Like, *babyish*?"

"It's Mozart," I told her distractedly, checking the screen. "Mozart composed this tune, which is genius in its simplicity."

Okay. It was a text from Payton, saying:

thx again for everything

"Cool factoid," Ox said, nodding at me.

"Whatever, Payton," Sydney said. Her face said, *Leave already*.

"It's okay," I said. "Sydney can have the seat." And Payton could stay on Sydney's good side.

Sydney smiled. But then—

"Dude," some guy behind us said. "Tell your girlfriend to sit down and stop blocking us. We can't see the cheerleaders."

The cheerleaders were flipping and kicking out on the gym floor. Sydney looked out at their performance and frowned. Then she turned back to me and said, "Buh-bye, Payton."

But I didn't move. Because Ox was holding the strap of my tote bag.

"Hey, Syd, look." Ox pointed. "There's an empty seat in the back next to Cashmere. I'll see you later."

Sydney glared at me.

"You—you—," she sputtered, and then *BAM!* A stray pompom flew toward us and whapped Sydney smack in the face.

"Eck! Blecch!" Sydney gagged, pulling green and white strips from her mouth.

"Hey, Cindy!" one of the cheerleaders called. "Can I have that back?"

"Augh!" Sydney yelled, and threw the pompom down. Then she stomped off.

Ox let go of my bag. "C'mon," he said to me. "Sit."

I sat. On a pompom. I handed it to Ox, who threw it right to the cheerleader who'd lost it. *Good aim,* I thought, watching the pompom. *Nice muscles,* I thought, peeking at Ox's throwing arm.

I didn't bother turning around to see Sydney's walk of shame back up the bleachers.

Sorry, Payton. I did my best to salvage your relationship with Sydney. It's her loss.

I looked at Ox. *And my gain.* I was sitting so close to him that if I moved a teensy bit over, we'd be touching. I felt all tingly just thinking about it. I pretended to listen to the football coach talking about the season. But I was really thinking about . . .

Ox.

"Good cheerleading," Ox whispered to me.

"What?"

"You, leading the Gecko Finger Cheer," he said. "Thanks for showing our team school spirit. I was psyched that I found you."

"Er, thanks," I said. *Well*. I'd never been called a good cheerleader before.

My brain felt all swirly. I sneaked a look at Ox, who was now focused on the football coach. I had him for just one day. I felt like Cinderella. When the dismissal bell rang, I'd have to turn back into . . . myself. Emma.

The coach stopped talking and the lights turned off.

And suddenly there was something on the big movie screen.

"Good afternoon, Geckos!" A huge Jazmine James face appeared. She was sitting at a news desk. "Welcome to the first broadcast of VOGS, for students and by students. I'm Jazmine James, this week's host."

Bleh. A huge, giant Jazmine James. I sneaked another look at Ox. I'd rather look at him. And his huge, giant muscles you could see rippling through his shirt sleeves, and—

"Hey, there's your sister!" Ox nudged me. It was! Payton was up on the screen! Woo-hoo! Go, Payton! I mean, go, Payton-Emma! Go, me!

"Hi! I'm Emma Mills!" she said with a smile. "With your special Gecko pep rally report."

Yay! There she was. Reporting live on camera. And she was doing well. Really well. She was talking about the game tonight.

"Are you guys ready for the big game tonight?" she said. And then she stood up and cheered. "GECK!"

And the whole audience screamed back, "O! GECK! O!"

"Tell her she should try out for basketball cheerleading," Ox said.

I was so proud of her. I listened to her talk about the game tonight.

"Hey, isn't that your wrist thingy she's wearing?" Ox asked me.

What?

I looked up at the screen. Oh, no. She was wearing her *P* cuff. I looked down. I was wearing my *E*. We'd forgotten to trade in that last switch.

"Heh," Ox said. "I know people mix you up, but it's like even you don't know who's who."

Ha ha ha. I smiled weakly. Yikes. Well, it was only one little mistake. (Blown up to about one hundred times its normal size on a giant screen.) I looked around, hoping nobody would notice.

And then some boy came on to talk about bus safety. Whew. Payton was done! Over! She'd done great! But I was relieved it was over. There was no longer anything to worry about.

Jazmine's face came back on the screen.

"And now for our student spotlight," Jazmine said. "Every week we'll surprise a student by putting them in the spotlight. This week, our surprise student spotlight is . . . Emma Mills!"

Something to worry about! Something to worry about!

The camera panned out to show both Jazmine and Payton behind the long desk. Payton looked stunned.

"So, Emma," Jazmine said. "Thanks for joining us for our first-ever surprise student spotlight! How do you like being a Gecko?"

"Um," Payton said. "It's great?"

"Emma Mills was last year's state spelling champion," Jazmine said. "Emma, can you share your winning word with us?"

"Um . . ." Payton's forehead crinkled.

Logorrhea, I willed her to answer. *Logorrhea.*

If twin ESP were ever true, please let it work now.

And then she smiled and sat up straighter. Phew! It worked! She remembered it!

"Diarrhea!" she said, brightly. "It was diarrhea!"

People in the audience cracked up. Oh, no.

"Interesting," Jazmine said. "Well, you're also an elementary school mathletics champion, like I was. And I can see why! Here's an example of Emma's work. *P* equals *E*, and *E* equals *P*."

Huh?

And then Jazmine held up a piece of paper. It was Payton's copy of the switch schedule I had made.

Oh. NO.

Jazmine knew.

Jazmine knew. And Payton was up there with no idea.

"I—I—" I turned to Ox. "I have to go."

"You have to go?" Ox asked.

No time to explain. I got up.

"Down in front!" the annoying kid behind me hissed.

I leaned down. And crawled out of the assembly as fast as I possibly could. And ran to the VOGS studio.

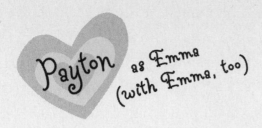
Payton as Emma
(with Emma, too)

Twenty-five

STILL NINTH PERIOD

"Yes! That's right! I love science, too!" I said. "That's me! Science fair . . . lover!"

This was way awkward. Here I was, sitting on camera while Jazmine James interviewed me as Emma. Why, oh, why did they have to choose me as the first student spotlight? I didn't know the answers to these questions.

"So you have a twin sister, Payton," Jazmine said.

"Yes!" I nodded. "Payton is . . . great! She's a great twin!"

"And she must be so supportive of you," Jazmine continued. "Because she's here in the studio right now!"

Jazmine pointed off camera. Emma! Emma was there?

"Emma—Pay—?" I stammered. "I mean, Payton-mma! I mean . . . PAYTON! Hi, TWIN!"

Okay, that was smooth.

Emma was giving me looks. Looks that meant . . . I didn't know what she was trying to tell me. *Use your twin ESP, Emma! I don't understand!*

"Why, they look like clones," Jazmine said into the camera. I saw Emma's face freeze as she was on-screen. Then the camera swung back to me. "Except that Emma's nose is bigger."

No, actually my nose was bigger. But if this was going to be broadcast to the entire school, I guess I'd rather have that mixed up.

"And now it's time for our weather report! Adam, over to you!"

Some guy's face filled the screen on the camera, with a large map behind him. Whew. I was glad that was over.

"Thanks for the interview, *Emma*," Jazmine said. "Or wait, are you Payton? It's *so* easy to get you two mixed up. Have you ever traded places?"

Huh? I looked at Emma. She looked frozen.

"No, I'm sure you would *never* do that," Jazmine cooed. "That would be dishonest, wouldn't it? Especially for Emma, an honors student who is likely hoping to represent the school in so many competitions?"

Emma looked down at the floor.

"Well! I'd better get ready for my next segment!" Jazmine said. She practically skipped away.

"She knows!" Emma hissed at me. "Jazmine knows we switched places!"

She knows?

"And," Emma continued, panicky, "she's going to tell on us!"

"Why would she do that?" I asked her.

"Why? Why? Because I'm a threat to her! She knows I—I, Emma—am competition in the spelling bee! Mathletes! Science fairs!" Emma was in a panic now. "It's her chance to take down the competition!"

Oh. Yeah. That.

"Somehow she got our switched schedule," Emma kept going. "I still have my copy. How could she have gotten hold of the *only other copy* of the schedule?"

???
???

Oh. *She must have gotten it when I knocked into her and all our stuff got mixed up on the floor.*

"Um—," I started to say, but Emma cut me off.

"I give you one easy task—not to lose the schedule! How could you be so dumb?"

Dumb? Did Emma just call me dumb?

"Excuse me, Miss Brainiac," I told her. "I know I'm not as smart as you are, but at least I can go on camera. And make you look good!"

"Make me look good?" Emma said. "You just told everyone I won the spelling bee with the word 'diarrhea'!"

"I was helping you out!" I protested.

"I sacrificed my crush so you could have your so-called friends," Emma said. "Your superficial, shallow, clothes-obsessed popular people!"

"Like your 'we're too smart to have any fun' brainiac people are any better?" I shot back. "You're so selfish!"

"Selfish!" Emma practically screamed. "After everything I've done for you?!"

She raised her hand. Was she going to . . . smack me?

And all of a sudden I realized that the room had gone quiet. I looked down at my shirt. Oh, no. My microphone was still attached.

I looked up at the VOGS monitor. Emma and I were on camera.

We were on camera.

"Emma," I said, slowly. "Um."

I pointed.

Emma looked over and saw herself on camera. Both of our faces, in total shock, were being broadcast to the entire student body.

Please tell me our entire fight was not just broadcast to the entire school.

I looked around and saw all the news reporters staring at us.

Oh, no. It was.

The camera turned, and Jazmine was back on-screen.

"Wow!" Jazmine said, from behind the desk. "That was enlightening! We almost had that twin question answered, didn't we: If one twin slaps the other in the face, will the other one feel it?"

Emma slowly put her hand down. We looked at each other in horror.

"Thanks, Emma and Payton—or should I say Payton and Emma?" Jazmine said, cheerfully. "What a fascinating inside look at twins! And that's our show for the day."

She turned and smiled at us.

Emma looked at me. I looked at Emma.

"And, cut!" the producer said. "It's over!"

It was.

It was over.

For the Mills twins, that is.

Emma

Twenty-six

IN THE CAR

Principal Patel had called our parents into school after the VOGS incident. Two long, humiliating hours later we were in the car on our way home.

I was sitting in the middle seat. Payton was sitting in the back.

"Grounded," Dad said. "Both of you. For a month. No, two."

"I just don't understand what you two were thinking," Mom said. "Especially you, Emma. You've always had such a good head on your shoulders."

BRRRZPP!

I had a text message. From Payton.

And what's mine? A bad head?

I almost smiled at Payton's text. But I stopped myself. I was still too mad at her to reply.

"How is this going to look on your permanent records?" Mom said. "Detention!"

I groaned. What college would want me now? Who would want such a troublemaker? All my hard work had been destroyed, all because Payton wanted to be popular!

I texted Payton:

This is all ur fault.

There. Now I was never going to speak—or text—my sister again. I put my phone away.

"And the manipulation, the deception . . . ," my mother droned on.

"The principal said it's lucky you didn't take any tests for each other, or you'd have been suspended for cheating," Dad said. "Or even expelled!"

Sheesh, it's not like we broke the law or anything. I sneaked a look at Payton in the rearview mirror. She looked as miserable as I felt.

"Both of you betrayed people," my mother said.

"You've disappointed us, and you've disappointed people at your new school. What are you going to do about it?"

What are we going to do about it?

"I know what I'm going to do about it," Payton said. "I'm going into the witness protection program."

"Haven't you had enough identity switching?" Mom asked.

"Fine, then I'm switching schools," Payton grumbled.

"Young lady, you are not switching anything. You are going to face the consequences," Dad said.

"My future is over," Payton sighed.

Hmm. That gave me an idea. We couldn't change the past, but maybe—just maybe—we could make things a little better at school.

Last weekend we'd practiced becoming each other. Now we had to prepare for something else: being ourselves (our humbled, humiliated selves).

I texted her.

We need 2 do live apology on VOGS 2 the school.

Payton's head popped over the seat.
"Seriously?" she whispered.

I nodded. It was the only way I could think of to do damage control.

"YOU want to go on camera?" Payton whispered.

"No," I whispered back, "I don't. But logically, it's the only reasonable solution. Plus, my phobia of being on camera was that I didn't want to look stupid. I kind of blew that already."

"Are you listening to us, girls?" my father yelled from the driver's seat.

Payton disappeared.

"Yes," we both said.

"You'd better listen, because blah blah blahbity blah . . ."

Hmm. The plan was beginning to percolate in my mind. It would take some work. We'd be up really late tonight. We'd have to figure out what we wanted to say to everybody. As well as do the extra assignments that the principal had told our teachers to give us. But what else did we have to do? We were grounded. No TV. No computer. Aaugh!

At least we'd be together. Like we were back in easier times. Before middle school, before Jazmine and Sydney and Ox.

Oh, Ox. It had been so great to be myself with a boy,

262

even if he'd thought I was somebody else. Well, life wasn't a fairy tale. I didn't get to magically switch places, destroy the evil witch(es), win the prince's heart, and live happily ever after. Reality was that Sydney and Jazmine and Ox would still be at school tomorrow. And we would have to face them all. As ourselves. Our true selves.

Payton

Twenty-seven

WEDNESDAY, HOMEROOM

The next morning, Emma and I convinced Dad to drive us in early. We went straight to Mrs. Burkle's classroom and explained what we wanted to do. She checked with Principal Patel. And our plan was put into action.

"At least that went well," Emma said as we walked out into the hallway. "At least she agreed we could do our own live VOGS special report. She didn't even sound mad at us."

"Yeah," I said. "She's probably the only one who isn't. It's going to be way hard to face everyone today."

"So we have five minutes at the end of the day to redeem ourselves," Emma said.

"It's going to be a long day until then," I said.

We reached our lockers.

"Well, Mrs. Burkle did say it was the most exciting live journalism she'd seen in a long time," Emma said.

"And the most embarrassing," I added. I opened my locker and started getting out my books.

Emma was looking at me.

"What?" I asked.

"Your tote bag." She pointed inside.

"I organized a little last night," I shrugged. Okay, maybe a lot. I'd gotten a few ideas from being Emma. "I put my books in order of my class schedule. And I'm going to use different color file folders like you do. For now, blue is Language Arts . . . and red is Social Studies. I'll have to buy the other colors when we're not grounded. Do you think yellow should be Art or—?"

"Whatever works for you," Emma said. "It's your system. Wow, *you* have an organizational system! I'm impressed."

I smiled. It was nice to impress Emma.

Emma reached into her backpack and got some things out. Including something blue and shiny that she was sticking up on her locker door.

"Hey, what's that?" I asked her.

"Nothing," Emma said.

"Yeah, if nothing equals cute locker decorations," I said. I peered in. Emma had just put up a locker-sized collage of blue and silver.

"That's really cute," I said.

"I borrowed some of Mom's scrapbooking stuff late last night. I couldn't sleep," Emma said. I watched as she put up some math symbol magnets—and a mirror. She checked her lip gloss and closed her locker.

"You are so Pay-tified!" I said. "I love it!"

"Well. Okay. Thanks," Emma said, looking a little embarrassed. "I'm going to homeroom. I can get some extra study time."

"Wait," I said. "Good luck today."

I held up my hand for the twin handslap. And we went off our separate ways.

I walked down the hall. I put my hands in my hoodie pockets, and in one I found a little blue sticky note.

It's great to be Emma,
but I'm "gray"-tful you're Payton!
:)

Aw. I smiled.

"Hey, it's one of those psycho twins," a boy said as he passed me.

My smile faded. I walked faster, my head down.

"Blah blah blah twins . . . blah blah hilarious . . . blah blah . . ." I tried to block out everybody's voice, and somehow I made it to homeroom.

The room got quiet as I walked in.

I kept my head down and walked quickly to my seat. Sydney was in her seat, and I avoided eye contact.

"Mills, Payton?" Mrs. Galbreath called out.

"Here," I said.

"Are you sure?" I heard Sydney whisper. "Maybe it's *Emma* Mills."

I cringed. The homeroom teacher kept on with her attendance.

I stared straight ahead. Unfortunately, the view was Sydney's shiny, perfect hair. I thought back to how badly I'd wanted to be friends with her. In a way, that had kind of started all of this.

"This is all because you wanted to be popular," Emma had hissed at me. Well, wait. *She* wanted to be popular too. It wasn't just me! We'd both wanted to be popular.

Sydney tossed a note to the girl sitting across from

her. The girl read the note and glanced at me. Then she laughed nervously.

Okay. I don't want to be that kind of popular. I was over scrubbing bathrooms and slaving for clothes, and I was over being nervous around Sydney, I decided. What I really wanted was some good friends.

Well. At least I had one true friend: Emma.

"Class, I need to step out for a minute," Mrs. Galbreath said. "Please study quietly at your desks."

She stepped out of the class. One second later the spitballs started flying. A crowd of groupies flocked to Sydney's desk.

I pretended to be fascinated with my math book. *La, la, la, not listening to them.*

"So. Payton."

Oh, no. Sydney had turned around and was facing me. As were the other girls, including Quinn.

"I feel so betrayed, Payton," Sydney said. "I was being a good friend to you, and you weren't even you. That is so wrong."

Everyone around her was like, *Yeah, so wrong.*

"I'm sorry," I said miserably. "I was just—"

"And I can't believe you thought that I would actually fall for it!" Sydney said. "Puh-lease. I knew all along."

What?

"Yeah," some girl echoed. "I mean, that Emma is in my science class, and she's a freaky brainiac."

"I know, right?" Sydney said. "Total geek. I mean, have you seen her sweatpants?"

"But you have to admit, your shirt is so way cute," Quinn said. "Emma did good there."

Huh?

"Um, what?" The words popped out of my mouth.

"You—I mean, Emma—picked out that shirt Sydney's wearing, when we went to the mall," Quinn said to me. "The saleslady was all like, 'Wow, Emma has mad cool taste.'"

Emma? My twin?

"And this!" Quinn continued, pointing to her necklace. "Isn't this cute? And all of Emma's new clothes when she was pretending to be you. Didn't Emma tell you that?"

Um, no. I thought back. I had assumed Sydney had picked out all the new clothes.

Emma did?

"Quinn! Jeesh! Shut it!" Sydney said, giving her a dirty look. "That is so not important."

Quinn's face fell.

"What is important," Sydney announced loudly, "is that Emma is a *loser*. And Payton is a *poser*."

Everyone looked at me. I felt like the whole world was looking at me. I felt my face turn bright red. I felt my heart pounding in my chest.

"Class!" The homeroom teacher walked back in. "People are out of their seats! I'm shocked! Return to your seats immediately!"

Sydney's friends scattered back to their desks. Sydney flipped her hair and turned back around facing front. But not before mouthing one word at me:

Poser.

I shrank down in my seat. My brain was a whirl. What would Emma do?

Doesn't matter. I'm Payton. What would Payton do? Payton would hide. As soon as homeroom was over, I walked quickly out of the classroom. And straight to the nurse's office.

"Name?" the nurse asked me.

"Payton Mills," I said.

"Have you been here before?" she asked, looking me up on her computer.

Um. Sort of. Under a different name.

"I guess not," I said.

❀ 270 ❀

"Problem?"

"I'm just—sick," I said.

"Your face *is* beet-red and flushed," the nurse announced. "And very sweaty. Likely a fever. Go lie down on the cot."

"Um, can you tell me when it's eighth period?" I asked. "I . . . I'll feel better by then."

"You know when you're going to feel better?" The nurse eyed me suspiciously.

Uh.

"Nurse! Nurse!" A teacher came running in, dragging a boy with her. "A student cut his finger!"

"It's just a paper cut," the kid said. "Jeez."

"We have a bleeder! We have a bleeder!" the nurse announced dramatically. "Everyone to a cot!"

The kid looked embarrassed but otherwise fine. I, on the other hand, was embarrassed and not fine. But at least I was forgotten. I took my sweaty red self over to the cot and lay down. I pulled the blanket over my face. I was just going to hide out here until it was time for our VOGS apology.

I wiggled around until I got more comfortable.

Mmmm . . . I had to admit that these capris I was wearing—which Emma had picked out at the mall—

were pretty soft and comfy. Trendy and comfy. No more uncomfortable Summer Slave clothes, I decided.

Well, except for the yellow cami—that was really cute. Oh, and the gray sweater was a little itchy, but totally worth it. And when my feet grew a little bigger, I was definitely going to wear those platforms, and—

Zzzzz

Zzzzzzz

zzzzzzzzzzzzzzzzzzzz

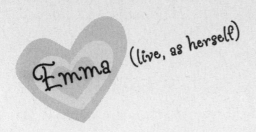

Twenty-eight

NINTH PERIOD

Finally, it was last period. I sat down in math class and looked at the clock. I had twenty minutes of Math, and then it was off to the VOGS studio.

"Oh, look, it's the diarrhea twin. Is it really her or is it her sister?" Jazmine announced as she walked in.

I heard Hector laugh, but I didn't look up from my book.

"I think I should win a middle-school journalism award for my exposé. I'll just put it in my display case next to all my other awards." Jazmine's voice carried across the room.

I ignored Jazmine, as I had all day. She must have spent all night thinking of put-downs for me. Sure, Mrs.

Burkle had given her a talking-to about putting us on camera without us knowing; sure, she wasn't allowed to be anchorperson as a consequence. That didn't seem to be bothering Jazmine, who was probably just eating up the attention. I mean, the incident had practically made her famous in school.

I, on the other hand, was infamous. And in nineteen minutes I would be more so.

I watched Jazmine talking to Hector and Tess, and for a moment I felt a pang of envy.

Whatever, I told myself. *I'm Emma. I don't have time for friends. I'm all about the studying.*

"You know what would be weird?" a girl sitting next to me said to her friend. "I wonder if they ever switched places on their boyfriends."

"Awesome," said the guy next to them. "The guy would have like two girls."

"Ew," the girl said, giggling.

Doesn't anyone have a life? Ugh. I continued studying, like *those* people should. *If x is a square root and y is Pi* . . . Augh! I couldn't concentrate.

I thought about what the girl had said. . . . *If they ever switched places on their boyfriends?* Well, we'd never had boyfriends, now, had we? But I'd almost had a chance. Ox

was almost going to maybe have been my boyfriend . . .
even if he thought I was really Payton.

*Oh, let's face it. I'm not ever going to have a boyfriend.
Who'd want to date boring Emma?* Ugh. Ugh. Ugh!
Before this switch, I'd liked myself! I was smart, confi-
dent, intelligent, focused.

But . . . before the switch, I was also stressed out and,
well, pretty much having no fun. And no Ox. I hadn't
known what I was missing.

Now I was missing Ox. Who would never talk to me
again.

I'd seen him twice today in the halls. But each time
I'd seen him coming, I'd walked quickly the other way. I
mean, what could I say to him? And worse, what would
he want to say to me?

I remembered how we'd talked about ox trivia. And
how he'd smiled at me a lot. It was like he got me. Emma
me. Not Payton me. Or spelling-bee/mathlete/competi-
tion me.

Just me.

Sigh.

The math teacher came in. I couldn't concentrate on
a word he said. Instead I watched the clock. Seventeen
minutes . . . sixteen . . . ten . . . five . . .

And then it was time to go.

I took a deep breath, got up, and handed my math teacher the pass. And went to the media room to meet Payton.

I walked into the media room. The studio was busy with people on the equipment, but I didn't see Payton anywhere. Mrs. Burkle came over to me.

"Emma!" she said. She sounded a little too cheerful. "You have ten minutes till airtime. This is so very exciting! Our first special report! I'd dreamed of having the opportunity to break into regularly scheduled classes. But I didn't know it would happen so soon in the year!"

She walked away gleefully, directing the camera people around.

"She's picturing good ratings," one of the camera people said to me. It was Nick, the guy who sat behind me in homeroom.

"I'm glad someone is happy about this," I said to him miserably.

"She's probably thinking it will get her a raise. It's like our own school reality show," Nick said. "Starring the Switching Twins. She'll probably put it on YouTube."

Gee. Great. I usually liked to please my teachers, but this wasn't what I'd had in mind.

"Nick!" Mrs. Burkle sang out. "Camera two needs you!"

Nick rolled his eyes and walked away.

Just then Payton walked in, all out of breath.

"Hey," she said, "I almost couldn't get here. My PE teacher didn't believe I was really excused. 'How do I know I can trust you?' she said. Ugh."

"Bummer. So how was the rest of your day?" I asked her.

"Exhausting," she said. "Yours?"

"Heinous," I replied. And it was only about to get worse. I was going on camera soon.

Nick came over to us.

"Um, hi, Nick," Payton said, hesitantly.

"So," Nick said impersonally, "do you want to both be on at the same time, or will we shoot you individually?"

Just shoot me now. Get this over with.

"Together," I said out loud.

"Two minutes!" Mrs. Burkle said. "Places, people!"

She shuffled Payton and me over to the big desk in front of the cameras. I sat down.

And reality sank in.

"Payton," I said, "I can't do this. I'm having an attack. An attack of extreme technocameraphobia, which can manifest as seizures, frozen limb syndrome, or otolaryngitis."

"Sorry," Payton said. "I've already had otolaryngitis, and let me tell you, it doesn't get you excused from things."

I chewed my hair. I wasn't kidding, though. I was seriously nervous.

"Stop chewing." Payton leaned over and pulled my hair out of my mouth. "You can't freak out. We rehearsed this at least five thousand times. We both know exactly what we're going to say."

She was right. My nerves might have been shaky, but my memory would never fail me.

"Time to hook up your mikes," Mrs. Burkle said. "We want to hear every word you say!"

She attached a tiny microphone to my collar and another to Payton's cami strap.

"Your clothes look cute," I told Payton.

"I still can't believe *you* picked them out." She shook her head. "You have this secret inner fashionista and I have to find out from the Sydney crew? Weird. You look cute too."

Okay, so I was wearing my hair down instead of back in the old ponytail. And I'd applied some hair shine and lip gloss. A little effort on my part didn't detract from my intelligence, I'd decided.

But I was keeping the T-shirt and the sweats. They were part of what made me me. Okay, I'd upgraded the sweats to cute little track pants instead of floppy ones. But still. I was still me in them.

"One minute till our special report!" said Mrs. Burkle. "Breaking into all the classrooms, LIVE!"

The room lights dimmed. Except for one in the middle, which shone a spotlight on Payton and me.

"Quiet on the set!"

No problem there. My brain and mouth had frozen up.

"Three . . . two . . . one . . . action," said Nick, aiming the camera.

A few bars of our school song played. Then there was silence.

"Welcome to a special edition of VOGS," said Payton, like a pro. "I'm Payton Mills."

"And I'm Emma Mills," I managed to squeak out.

"As most of you know, we're the twins who switched places in school this week," Payton continued confidently. She was so good at this, I thought.

Pause.

Oh! Oops. My turn.

"That's right, Payton." I sounded stiff.

"We wanted everyone to know the truth," Payton

said. She leaned in closer to the camera. "The inside story of what really happened."

I noticed Mrs. Burkle clasping her hands with joy.

"The truth is that we were just going to switch for a couple of classes, and it was for a good cause," Payton explained. "I had an . . . emergency. An embarrassing-moment emergency. If it was in a Most Embarrassing Moments column in a magazine, it would have been a ten out of ten. But then Emma saved me."

"I offered to help her by taking her place." I recited my lines. "Just for a little while. It seemed like no big deal. Nobody would ever know."

"We never meant for it to get out of control," Payton said. "So we want to apologize to all of the students and faculty, and especially to all of our new friends."

I noticed the monitor off to the side of the room. It was showing the videocast. Except, wait . . .

"They mixed our names up!" I burst out.

"What?" Payton looked startled.

"Look! The names under us say that you're Emma and I'm Payton." I pointed to the monitor. Sure enough, the captions were mixed up.

"Stick to the script," my sister whispered.

"But wait—we're supposed to be showing everybody

our true selves, who we really are," I complained. "How do we do that with the wrong names under our faces?"

I mean, really. *Couldn't the person in charge of the captions have paid a little attention here?* I sighed.

"Well, you're doing a good job of showing everyone your obsessing picky self," Payton hissed.

"You mean that detail-oriented self?" I said. "The one that got your so-called friends to look so good at the mall? When I could have been doing something important like studying for a competition?"

"If I remember correctly, *you* were the one who ended up having fun at the mall," Payton said. "Because—"

Oh no. *Don't say because of Ox. Not live on VOGS. Don't say—*

"Because of reasons I won't name," Payton continued.

Phew. *Thanks, Payton, for not going there.*

"Besides, you liked the mall," Payton said. "I thought. You came home so happy."

"I did?" I thought about it. "Yeah, I did. I kind of realized that life doesn't always have to be serious, and that fashion can be, well, fun. Maybe not as fun as winning a science competition, of course, but . . . fun in a different way. You know, Payton, having fun and expressing yourself creatively, whether with art or music or even accessories, can be as important to the soul as any academic accomplishment."

I sat back, feeling oddly calm.

"Wow," Payton said. "That was deep."

"Thank you," I said, pleased.

"Emma's the smart one," Payton said, turning back toward the camera. "I have to confess that I got sucked into switching places because . . . well, I've always been the dumb twin. And when I was pretending to be Emma, people treated me like I was smart. And . . . I liked it."

"Well, being smart is cool, but being a nice person is even more important," I said. I stared at the camera, hoping Jazmine James was listening. "And Payton is one of the nicest people I've ever met."

"Aw, thanks, Emma," Payton said. "That's so sweet. But you know, when I was pretending to be you, I also learned that being smart can be mad cool. You get treated with more respect around here. You get special passes to the library."

I nodded. Too true.

"You know," Payton went on, "you even have to be in honors to do VOGS. Seriously, does that seem fair? I mean, I really loved doing VOGS, and now I won't be able to do it. Well, for one thing because we have detention and I'm grounded for the rest of my life. But none of us non-honors people get to be on TV. That's sad."

"Ahem." I heard someone clear her throat. It was Mrs. Burkle, looking slightly stunned at this turn of events.

"Twenty seconds!" Nick whispered from behind the camera. Oh! Our time was almost up!

"So just think about if you had the chance to be someone else for one day," I said into the camera. This was from our script, but . . . I truly meant it. "Wouldn't you maybe try it out?"

"Seriously, we are way sorry if we confused anyone or made you mad," Payton said. "We really made some good friends out there, and things just got a little crazy."

"And now we just want things to get back to normal," I added. "We just want to be ourselves. This is Emma Mills."

"And Payton Mills. Signing off for this special edition of VOGS."

I sat there with a stupid grin on my face, waiting for the camera's red light to go off. *Still waiting*. It was totally silent. Uh . . . was I supposed to say something now? I opened my mouth:

"Go, Geckos!" I said.

And the red light went out.

"Go, Geckos?" Payton said. "What was that?"

❀ 283 ❀

"I choked! I panicked! Why didn't the red light go off?"

"Uh . . . because we were rolling out the credits," Nick said, peering out from behind the camera.

"Oh. Okay. Phew. That means no one heard me at the end, right?" I asked.

"Actually, the audio was still on," Nick said. "So everyone in the school heard you."

Payton let out a snort.

"Are you laughing at me?" I demanded.

"'This is Emma "The Brain" Mills, signing off.'" Payton giggled. "'Go, Geckos!'"

It was pretty funny.

I smiled.

"Nice work, Mills." Mrs. Burkle came over. "And you too, Mills. Had all the ingredients for a compelling broadcast—mystery! Intrigue! Remorse! Humor! School spirit!"

We held it in until she walked away. Then Payton and I looked at each other. And we both burst out laughing until we were practically rolling on the floor.

Okay, yeah, we screwed up, and maybe nobody would talk to us again. But we had each other. And nothing could break our twin bond.

Payton

Twenty-nine

WEDNESDAY, END OF THE SCHOOL DAY

"Okay, yeah, we screwed up, and maybe nobody will talk to us again," Emma said to me. "But we have each other. And nothing can break our twin bond."

Awwww. That is so sweet! And so . . .

Wrong. I mean, no offense, Emma, twin bonds are great, but I definitely want people to talk to me again!

"Hey, Mills twins." Nick came over from behind the camera. "Nice job."

"Thanks," we both said. At exactly the same time.

"And hey, Payton," Nick said. "All that about you not being smart? What you've done with VOGS is definitely smart stuff."

"Thanks!" I said. By myself this time.

Nick gave us a wave and walked away.

"Yay! Someone talked to us," I said.

"He seems nice," Emma said.

"Yeah," I said. "I actually had him picked out for you as your future boyfriend. He seems like your type."

"He does," Emma said. "But . . ."

I knew what she was thinking. Football jock Ox didn't seem like her type. But he was.

". . . he seems like a good friend for you," Emma finished.

"Yeah," I said. One friend. Better than zero friends.

Clang!

The end of the school day.

"Time for our after-school, er, meeting," I said. "Otherwise known as detention."

"I cannot believe that I, Emma Mills, have to go to detention," Emma grumbled.

"At least it's only a couple of days," I said. "Then we do community-service hours."

We walked around a corner. And smack into Quinn.

"Hi," Quinn said.

"Uh, hi," Emma said. "Look, I'm really sorry about switching."

"I saw you on VOGS," Quinn said. "And really, I get it. Some days I feel like trading places with someone else, too."

Her cell phone rang.

"Yeah, Sydney, I'm coming. I had to stop at my locker! Look, I'm sorry!" Quinn's voice was rising. She shut her phone. "As I was saying, some days I *realllllly* feel like trading places with someone else."

Emma and I looked at each other. Well, at least I wouldn't have Sydney pressure anymore.

"Apparently, I'm late," Quinn said, rolling her eyes. "Can't be late for another day of shopping, can I?"

She started walking away and then turned around.

"Um, hey," she said. "So, Emma, you're the one who went to the mall with us, right?"

Emma nodded.

"I had fun with you. I don't know if . . . do you want to maybe hang out sometime?" Quinn asked hesitantly. "I mean, I don't know if you're okay doing something other than shopping. I'm trying to save up for a new laptop, but I keep blowing my money at the mall. Do you like to do anything besides shop?"

I looked at Emma. Emma looked at me.

Did Emma like to do anything besides shop? Gee. I tried not to crack up.

"Yes," Emma said. "I like to do lots of things besides shop."

"Cool!" Quinn said. "I'll give you my number."

Emma took out her turquoise-sparkly cell phone and put in Quinn's info. Quinn said bye, and we continued walking.

"You go, girl!" I said to Emma. "You have a friend! That is, if you can break out of your fashionista mode."

"Funny," Emma said. She was smiling. Then she stopped smiling. "What do you think she'd want to do if we hung out? Scrabble? Pictionary? Trivial Pursuit: Genius Edition?"

"Chill, Emma," I interrupted. "Try a movie first, 'kay?"

We turned another corner. And ran smack into Jazmine James. As usual, she was flanked by Tess and Hector.

"Well, if it isn't Double Trouble," Jazmine said. "Are you on your way to the History Club meeting? Oh, no, wait—you can't. You're going to detention."

Hector snorted.

I looked down. I didn't even want to see what Emma's face looked like.

And then suddenly Tess spoke up.

"I liked your TV interview," Tess said. "Both of you.

But Payton, you're a really impressive communicator."

"Um, thanks?" I said. Emma grinned at me.

"That's the second great speech you've given," Tess said. "First the one in Math, and now the one on TV."

"Oh!" I said. "Thanks!"

"What do you mean, 'great speech'?" Jazmine said dismissively. "She was just apologizing for playing tricks on all of us. Well, except me, of course, since I was the only one who noticed the obvious."

Harsh.

"Well." Tess looked at Jazmine. "For one thing, I liked when Payton said that. I agree with that one hundred percent. Payton, can I have your cell number? If it's okay, I'd like to call you sometime soon." She entered my phone number in as I told her the numbers.

Then Tess looked at Jazmine. Jazmine looked at Tess. Jazmine had a scowl on her face. Tess didn't flinch.

"Oooh!" Hector said. "A showdown! Let the drama begin!"

"Did someone say drama?" a loud voice boomed, making us all jump.

Mrs. Burkle!

"If there's drama around, I want it for the next edition of VOGS!" Mrs. Burkle said. "We need to keep our audience interested. Keep up the excitement level after today's compelling show!"

Mrs. Burkle looked at Emma and me.

"I have an idea for next week for you two," she said to me and Emma. "You can do a special report together, and—"

"Excuse me," Jazmine said, in her sucking-up-to-teacher voice. "I don't mean to be disrespectful, but as Payton is not an honors student, she's ineligible to be involved with VOGS."

I felt my face get red.

"What? Who makes these rules? That is outrageous!" Mrs. Burkle shouted. "Wait! I make these rules! Thus, I can change them! VOGS will now be open to all students. I will hold auditions to find the best dramatic talent!"

Really?

"Payton, consider your show today an audition!" Mrs. Burkle said. "And you have made it. Congratulations."

"Really?" I said. "Oh, my gosh. That's so cool!"

"What?" Jazmine said. "You're opening it up to anyone? It should be exclusive!"

"We will exclude some persons!" said Mrs. Burkle. "Attitude will be considered during auditions. We will see if you can check yours at the audition, Ms. James."

"What?" Jazmine said. "*I* have to audition?"

"Look for the sign-up sheet," Mrs. Burkle said.

Jazmine stomped away.

"Hector! Tess! History Club, now!" Jazmine said as she left. Then we heard her say, "Hector, stop laughing. It's *not* funny." The three walked away.

My cell phone went off.

i think i'll try out 2. Maybe u can help me practice? U r really good. xo Tess

I smiled.

"Well, let's go," I said.

"Did you see the look on Jazmine's face when Mrs. Burkle told her she had to audition?" Emma said. "Ha! That was classic. But that Tess seems nice. Wonder why she's always hanging around with Jazmine?"

"Maybe she didn't know she could make other friends," I said. But maybe she could now. Like me. Hee. I smiled.

And then my smile froze.

"Pay-EMMA! I mean, EMMA!" someone yelled down the hallway.

It was Ox.

I watched Emma's face turn purple, then an odd shade of white.

"Excuse me," I said quietly. I walked over to the other side of the hall to give them some privacy. Okay, no—actually, I still spied on them.

"I am so sorry—" Emma started to say, but Ox cut her off.

"Where have you been all day?" Ox said. "I was looking for you."

"Er, oh," Emma said. "Actually, whenever I saw you, I fled."

"Don't you think I deserved an explanation?" Ox asked her.

"I know, I know—I'm so sorry," Emma said. "I was so un-ox-like. I wasn't dependable or trustworthy, and not being honest with you was wrong. An ox is intelligent, and what I did was just dumb. So . . . I'm sorry."

Hello? What is Emma doing? I was about to break in and rescue her from geekiness, when I heard something unexpected.

Ox laughed.

"That was the most interesting apology I've ever heard," Ox said. "You are not exactly normal, you know."

We know, we know.

"I know," Emma said miserably. "That's why I wanted to switch with Payton. She's more normal and popular and all that. I wanted to see what it was like. But I can't be Miss Popularity or Miss Fashion-Obsessed. I just have to be myself."

"That's a relief," Ox said.

"It is?" Emma asked.

"Yeah. I've spent years trying to avoid Sydney and all those popular girls," Ox said. "Their conversations give me a headache. I'd rather not avoid you, too. So don't turn into that."

Ooooh! Oooooh!

I tried to send Emma twin ESP messages. *He likes you! Don't just turn purple! Say something!!!*

"I won't," Emma squeaked.

Yes! YEEESS! Go, Emma! Go, Emma!

"Good," Ox said. "Because I'd like to get to know Emma. Not the Emma-Payton hybrid. Just the real Emma."

Eeeee! He wanted to get to know Emma better! What would happen next? Maybe they would . . .

KISS!!!

I held my breath and waited in suspense. . . .

"Speaking of hybrids," Emma said, "did you know there are several kinds of bovine hybrids? For example, a yakow is a cross between a cow and a yak."

Uh.

That wasn't a kiss! Emma? What the heck are you doing?

"Yeah!" Ox said. "And a cross between a bison and a cow is a beefalo. And heh, have you ever heard of a zeedonk?"

"A zebra and a donkey!" Emma cried.

Oh. My.

I guess this was a perfect match.

Clang! The after-school warning bell!

Well, I hated to break up this romantic conversation, but . . .

"Ahem," I said as I started down the hall. "Emma. We'd better get to detention."

"Oh!" Emma snapped out of it. "Yes! Detention! Great!"

Oooh, boy. She had it bad.

"Yeah, I've got to go to pootball fractice," he said. "I mean—football practice!"

Hee! Ox was all flustered too!

"So I'll see you . . . ," Emma said. "Well, I guess I

won't see you at lunch anymore."

"Not unless you guys are planning more switching," Ox said.

"NO!" we both said.

"Then maybe I can see you at the football game Friday night, Emma," Ox said. "And afterward we all go out for pizza. Want to come with me?"

Emma nodded, but then . . .

"Oh, no—I'm grounded. But I'll talk to my parents. They're pretty cool, once they calm down."

"Well, if you can't get out, maybe we could have a phone date?" Ox asked. "After the game?"

"Okay!" Emma said.

Ox took off down the hall.

"Hey, Ox," Emma called out to him. He turned around.

"Go, Geckos!" she said. I saw him laugh.

Emma walked casually over to me. As soon as Ox disappeared around the corner, we screamed and jumped all around.

AHHHH!!! EEEEEEEEEEeeeee!

"Emma and Ox! Sitting in a tree!" I sang. "Talking about H-I-B-R-I-D-S!"

"Actually, it's spelled H-Y-B-R-I-D-S," Emma said.

"And hey! Were you spying on us?"

Oopsie.

"Maybe," I confessed. "Okay, yes."

"Well, at least you're honest about it," Emma said.

"I'm only going to be honest from now on," I pledged, "including about who I am. I'm Payton."

"And I'm Emma," Emma said. "We're never switching again!"

"That's right!" I agreed.

Emma and I held out our hands to do a TWIN-ky swear. But I didn't link pinkies.

"A TWIN-ky swear might be a little too . . . well . . . ," I said. "I mean, we can never, ever break a TWIN-ky swear."

"Yeah," Emma said. "It might be a little extreme to swear it off forever. Not that we're ever going to trade places again, right?"

"Never! Ever!" I said.

And we meant it. Then. But stuff happens, right? I guess you should never say never.

Top 10 Stupid Twin Questions People Ask

Answers by Payton and Emma

10. Are you two twins?

   Payton: Yes. (Duh, we look exactly alike.)

   Emma: Actually, we're clones.

9. Why aren't you dressed alike?

   P: Because . . . I have style? (Sorry, Emma. Kidding!)

   E: I have more important things to think about besides clothes. (Sorry, Payton!)

8. Do you talk in a secret twin language?

   P: Secret language? I can't understand Emma when she speaks English! My parents will be happy to tell you that she has a near-genius IQ. She's like a walking dictionary.

E: Ha. She can barely speak one language correctly. She thinks "yeesh" and "ew" are the most important words in the English language.

7. Do you ever switch places on your boyfriends?

P: Um, first we'd actually have to have boyfriends. Maybe this year? Please please please let me get a boyfriend this year! I think it's going to be a while for Emma. She turns purple and panics when she has to talk to a boy.

E: I do NOT! It's just that . . . I don't have time for a boyfriend. Yes, that's it. I'm too busy for boys. I'm going to sign up for Super Scientists Club, mathletics, school newspaper, piano, and Scrabble-lympics.

6. Do you ever forget which one you are?

P: Ew, no. Yeesh!

E: I don't forget anything. I have a near-photographic memory.

5. Which one of you is smarter?

P: See #8.

E: See #8.

4. If I smack you in the face, will your twin feel it?

P: Uh, I hope I never have to find out.

E: I'd rather not test that theory, thank you.

❀ 298 ❀

3. Which one of you is the evil twin?

    P: Neither of us is evil—right, Emma?

    E: Payton's not *really* evil. Just misguided by her peers and the media.

2. Do you guys read each other's minds?

    P: Heck, no. And take back that last thing you said about me, Emma. Whatever it means.

    E: No, we don't read each other's minds. I read books. She reads fashion magazines. (Ow, Payton, stop whacking me with that magazine!)

1. Do you like being an identical twin?

    P: Most of the time, except when Emma attempts her lame-o put-downs.

    E: Sorry, Payton, sometimes I just can't control myself. Ow! Stop whacking me. Yes, I do like it. Even with our differences, Payton and I are best friends.

    P: Yes. BTFF. Best twin friends forever!!!!

Acknowledgments

Double thanks to:

The family: Robin Rozines, Amy Rozines, Greg Roy, Dave DeVillers, and Quinn DeVillers.

The Simon & Schuster crew: Mark McVeigh, Ellen Krieger, and Alyson Heller of Aladdin, as well as Rick Richter, Bethany Buck, Mara Anastas, Karin Paprocki, Paul Crichton and his publicity team, Mary McAveney, Lucille Rettino and the marketing team, and Wendy Rubin.

The agents: Mel Berger and The William Morris Agency, Alyssa Eisner Henkin and Trident Media Group.

The fashion crew: Q, Ilana, and the Dipietra designers.

And: Lisa Yee, Melissa Wiechmann, Daphne Chan, Kay Panabaker, The Colonie Town Library, and everyone who's ever mixed us up, giving us good stories for this book.